Stanley's Bride

Book Six in the Millshore Brides
Kirsten Osbourne

Sign up for instant notification of all of Kirsten's New Releases here[1].

And

For a complete list of Kirsten's works head to her website wwww.kirstenandmorganna.com

---

1. http://www.kirstenandmorganna.com/newsletter

Chapter One

Stanley Gabriel was frustrated with life. He had three small children, and his wife had died just two years before while she was giving birth to little Charlotte. His wife had been Charlotte, so he'd given the baby her name.

At the time, it had felt like he was honoring his wife. Now he was just reminded of her death every day. Not that he wouldn't have thought about her every day anyway. His wife had been perfect in every way, and he missed her more than he had ever imagined possible.

His mother—bless her—watched the children while he farmed all day, and she usually sent supper home with him as well. He didn't know how she had the energy to help raise his children when she'd already raised too many of her own.

He dressed the children for church, wishing he knew how to fix the girls' hair. His oldest, Rachel, and his youngest were both girls. His only son was named Steven Edward after his father who died when Stanley was only fourteen years old.

Steven was much easier for Stanley than the girls. He had no idea what to do with girls. Rachel was six and had just started school at the schoolhouse in town. Steven and Charlotte stayed with his mother, and Rachel went to her house after school, instead of returning to her empty home.

As soon as the family arrived at church, Stanley looked for his mother. She always helped keep the children quiet while Pastor Jed spoke. His mother waved to him from where she was talking to Grace, Jack Smith's new bride. Grace had tried to get him to send for her best friend as a mail-order bride, but it just felt like he would be replacing the memory of a woman he'd loved for years with a stranger. How could that be right?

He walked toward his mother and Mrs. Smith, hoping the latter wouldn't start talking to him about her friend again. He might just break down and accept her idea, if only to have someone fix the girls' hair for church on Sundays.

He walked to the two women, leaning down to plant a kiss on his mother's cheek. "Good morning, Ma. Mrs. Smith." He looked behind him, but he saw Rachel had her siblings in hand, and they were already sitting down, ready for worship.

Ma looked at him for a moment. "Why have you not thought about getting yourself a mail-order bride, Stanley? You know how difficult you've had it since Charlotte died. It would solve so many problems."

Stanley sighed. He should have known. Just Mrs. Smith's presence turned the talk to mail-order brides. "Ma, you know I loved Charlotte so much. I can't imagine marrying a stranger and just hoping she'll be good with my children. And would accept the life of a woman who was married in name only so she could be a servant to her husband and his children."

Mrs. Smith's soft voice was the one that answered. "Sadie would have no problem with that. I've written her and explained the situation, but I also explained that you weren't interested in marriage with her."

"I asked you not to do that," Stanley said, frowning at the woman who couldn't seem to leave well-enough alone.

"You're not making sense, Stanley!" Ma replied. "Your life would be so much better if you had someone cooking, cleaning, and minding the children for you. I don't know why you don't just tell her that it will be a marriage in name only. That's how George and I started out, and it worked well for all of us."

Stanley nodded at the mention of his step-father, who had not only helped his mother out of a bind, but who had made her come alive again after they lost his father on the trail. "I don't know, Ma..."

"Well, I'm telling you now, it's worth trying. I'm not getting any younger, and if something were to happen to me, and your children were still depending on me for care all the time...well, you know as well as I do it would be a disaster."

Stanley closed his eyes for a moment before nodding reluctantly. He really couldn't continue to impose on his mother the way he had for two years already. "Send for her. I'll get a bank note for her trip out here tomorrow."

Mrs. Smith looked excited. "I'll wire her to get ready first thing in the morning. It takes two weeks for a letter to reach Massachusetts, but I'm sure she can leave immediately. I have an idea for that."

Stanley shrugged. "Whatever you need to do. I'll marry her when she arrives. How much should I send?"

Mrs. Smith named a figure that seemed very low to Stanley, but he wasn't about to complain. "All right. I'll take it to Ma's tomorrow, and you can get the bank draft from her."

Ma looked satisfied that he was finally agreeing. He knew he depended on her too much since Charlotte had died, but what else could he do?

He walked across the church and sat down with his children, taking Charlotte from her sister. He'd explain about the mail-order bride he was sending for later. For now, he would have to convince himself he was doing the right thing.

WHEN SADIE ARRIVED home from work Monday evening, there was a telegram waiting for her. She'd never received a telegram in her

life, and as she accepted the paper from Mrs. Durant, she said a silent
prayer that it was from Grace telling her she'd found her a husband.

Sadie and Grace had been best friends since the day Grace arrived
in the orphanage when she was three. Sadie had been left in a basket
there when she was just days old, and she was told that she'd been quiet
and withdrawn until Grace had arrived, crying for her mother every
night. Sadie had been there to comfort her friend, and when they'd
aged out of the orphanage, both of them had gone to work in the same
textile mill, weaving until their arms fell off.

She was feeling particularly sore that day, her shoulders throbbing
with the pain. She was ready to do anything to get away from the mill.
Well, not really anything, but close. She was a God-fearing woman, so
she wouldn't break His commandments to get away from the mill, but
she might think about it.

Her hand shook as she unfolded the single sheet of paper and read
the contents.

Dearest Sadie Stop

Stanley Gabriel has finally agreed to marry you Stop

*He intends to send $30 for your train fare and your needs on the
journey Stop*

*I suggest you borrow the money from Mrs. Durant and let her keep the
money he sends Stop*

*Then you can be here before fall comes and brings those cold winds
with it Stop*

Please leave as soon as you receive this wire Stop

Sadie's eyes were wide as she read the telegram once more. She
looked up at Mrs. Durant who was already nodding. "You should leave
on the first train in the morning."

Sadie stood for a moment, realizing the other girls' eyes were on
her. The girls that had come after they'd all started going west as
mail-order brides. She liked them all, but they were nothing like the

group of girls who had been there before. The girls she thought of as her sisters.

Tears were streaming down her face as she let out a loud whoop and hugged Mrs. Durant much tighter than she should have.

"I'm going to Clover Creek, and I'll get to spend time with Grace again. You have no idea how much I've missed her."

"I've seen it on your face every day, dear!" Mrs. Durant smiled. "We can't make you a dress before you leave like we did for Grace, but perhaps we could buy you a new bonnet?"

Sadie shook her head. "No, I don't want to waste any money. I don't really know what Mr. Gabriel's financial situation is, and I'd like to return as much of his money to him as possible."

"That's admirable. But remember, if you need something, that is what the money is for."

"I think I should go pack. I have so little, but still, going through my belongings will take a good long while." Sadie knew there were a few things she needed, but she would wait until she was in Washington Territory with Grace, the sister of her heart.

As Sadie hurried up the stairs, Mrs. Durant called, "Supper is ready!"

Sadie felt her face turning bright red. She knew they always had supper immediately after their shifts at the mill, but she'd totally forgotten in her excitement to quit her job and leave town immediately.

How glorious it would be not to have to sit behind a loom for hours and hours each day. Soon, she would do housework, cook, sew, and take care of children. Perhaps Mr. Gabriel wasn't excited about getting a new wife, but she was excited to be away from the mill and close to Grace once again.

Joining the others for supper, Sadie was quiet as the other women talked excitedly. It was going to be hard to leave them, even though she hadn't known them long. Hugging Grace would all be worth it though.

All the girls helped her go through her belongings that night, each of them helping her fold her clothing so that it wouldn't wrinkle as badly when they packed it in the old chest that every one of her belongings fit into.

It wasn't long before she was packed for her trip to her new home, which would be her last destination. She never planned to leave the little community Grace loved so very much. After all the newsy letters she'd received, she felt as if she knew everyone in the community anyway.

"We're going to miss you," Mary said. "Especially on Wednesday nights."

Sadie laughed softly, remembering the little poetry club she'd had such a passion for at one point. She still enjoyed her writing, but more than anything she preferred to write prose and not poetry. "Well, now no one has to feel guilty if they don't want to attend."

All of the girls laughed softly at that, but Sadie knew. Once Cecelia had left, it didn't feel as if the club mattered at all. She'd tried to keep it going in honor of her friends who had moved on, but it just wasn't the same, and she'd talked with the girls or spent her time crafting some of her stories in memory of good times with friends.

"I'm glad I was able to get to know all of you, and I hope you'll write. Not poetry, of course, but letters. Letters will tell a story of the lives you're leading and how you're doing. I will endeavor to write each of you at least once per month. Will you write me back?"

The other girls nodded, a couple of them reluctantly. That was all right with Sadie, though. A reluctant promise was still a promise.

With her trunk beside her bed, Sadie fell asleep, hearing the sounds of the other girls sleeping around her. In the morning, when they headed for the mill, she would be on a train headed to Clover Creek in Washington Territory to meet the man she would spend the rest of her life with. Sure, it wasn't as romantic as it sounded, but she would still find romance in life, even if Mr. Gabriel refused to do the same.

She would have a home she could call her own for the first time in her life. Sadie was officially going to be a married lady.

THE TRAIN RIDE FELT like it took years, but really was only about two weeks, which was a miraculously short amount of time to get almost completely across America.

When the train pulled into Clover Creek station, Sadie got to her feet, took her small bag she'd taken onto the train with her, and went to the doors to see her new world. Everything she ever needed would be right there in the small town Grace already called home.

She wasn't surprised to see Grace standing on the platform looking for her. Sadie didn't care if it was ladylike or not. When she saw her friend, she ran straight toward her, bursting into tears. "It's been too long to be without my very best friend in the world," she said, weeping into Grace's shoulder.

Grace clutched her and wept as well. "I have missed you every single day we've been apart."

"And I you." Sadie pulled back and looked at her friend from head to toe. Her burgeoning belly changed her friend's shape, but not her face. "You're huge! Are you sure it's not twins?"

"Bite your tongue, Sadie! Jack's sister has three sets of twins, and I'm afraid I may follow suit."

"Yes, but if you had twin girls, you could name them Sadie and Grace, and it would be like we were watching ourselves grow up all over again."

Grace laughed, shaking her head. "No. The plan is for each of us to have a little girl, and the two of them can be the best of friends."

Sadie smiled, liking the idea of that even more than she liked the idea of Grace having twins. "Did you drive yourself?" She looked around, wondering if Stanley had come to meet her, or if she would meet him later.

"Jack barely lets me drive when I'm not expecting," Grace responded. "Now that I am, he wants to put me on a high shelf where no one can hurt me, and I can just grow his baby."

Sadie laughed. "Does he not realize how you've had to take care of yourself over the years?"

"He does know. And he wants to make up for every bad moment I've had in my entire life. He's a good man, Sadie. You're going to like him."

"Am I going to like Mr. Gabriel?"

Grace sighed. "I'm honestly not sure. But I know he needs you, even if he doesn't want you." She saw Jack approaching with Sadie's trunk and whispered, "We'll talk about it when we get home. I figured you'd want to be cleaned up before you met your future husband."

"He knows I'm arriving today?" Sadie asked, praying that he did.

"He knows. He won't have time to marry until Saturday though. You'll stay with me until then, and we'll talk and talk, like we used to." Grace linked arms with Sadie, and they walked toward the wagon together.

"I think that's a wonderful plan. Then we can have some time together, and I can get to know your Jack a little."

"It's going to be just like old times," Grace said.

Chapter Two

S adie couldn't help but fall a little in love with Grace's home. It was so picture perfect in Sadie's eyes. Never in her life had she had a home of her own, and here her friend was, the mistress of the cutest house she'd ever seen.

She was given a bedroom upstairs to use, down the hall from Grace and Jack's room. And there was a nursery set up between the two rooms. Sadie knew she needed to make something to add to the pretty little room, but she'd have to think about what it should be.

It was still morning, and apparently Grace and Jack hadn't had breakfast before going to the train station, so Sadie put her apron on and went downstairs to help her friend with the meal.

Grace shook her head adamantly. "I remember how tired I was after that train ride. You just sit, and I'll cook."

Sadie felt bad doing as her friend said. "But you're expecting."

"It's a perfect normal condition for a woman. Why I've heard stories of Indians who had the baby and just went on with their workday like it was nothing."

Sadie shook her head. "You do remember you're not an Indian, right?"

Grace laughed. "I do remember!"

Jack came into the house then with a pail of milk. "Fresh from the cow!"

"Just how we like it around here."

Jack washed his hands and joined Sadie at the kitchen table. "So what do you think of Clover Creek so far?"

"It's beautiful!" Sadie said. "I was expecting it to be colder, but it's downright pleasant outside."

Jack laughed. "It's only September. By January, you'll be begging for all the snow to melt!"

"Are there fun things to do in the winter?" Sadie asked.

"Sledding is a great deal of fun, but you shouldn't go when you're pregnant." Grace's eyes met Jack's, and Sadie knew they were each thinking of a shared memory. "I like going for sleigh rides as well. We have church socials most Saturday nights in the winter. We all dance and carry on and have a great deal of fun."

"Oh, that does sound fun." Sadie looked forward to the church socials. For a moment, her mind drifted to meeting a man she could fall in love with, and then she remembered that she would be marrying on Saturday. "What can you tell me about Mr. Gabriel?"

"Stanley? He's a great guy. We were in the same company coming west. Well, we were after we found him, his mother, and his siblings at the side of the trail. I was young when we came west, but I still remember watching Stanley drive his family's wagon and thinking I wanted to be as big and strong as Stanley was one day. Both his family and mine started out with two parents going west. Unfortunately, I lost both parents, and Stanley lost his father, leaving him the man of the family until his mother remarried a few months later."

"Months? I know it took a long time to go west in the wagons, but it was really months?"

Jack laughed. "We left Independence, Missouri in March of 1852, and we arrived here just in time to get shelter built before winter. Of course, we made it all the way to Oregon City to file our claims as part of that time."

"It never occurred to me it was that long. I was thinking weeks." Sadie shook her head, thinking about the hardship the people on the trail must have faced. "What was the town like when you first arrived?"

He shook his head with a small smile. "It was a large meadow. We all fell in love with the peacefulness here, and we'd already all decided to settle together, so we chose this to be our homes. Every building you see was built by the hands of someone on that wagon train."

"Wow. I'm sure some people have moved into town?"

Jack nodded. "Oh, yes, of course. We were right on the Oregon Trail, so people would see the town as they camped here, and many families decided to join us here in our own little paradise. I don't know if Grace has told you but there's a lake not far from here that's just beautiful. It's called Bear Lake, and our little area here is called Bear Lake Valley."

"The mountains are just beautiful. I've never lived so near something quite so majestic."

"You two have pretty much always lived together, right?" he asked.

Grace nodded. "From the time I was three when my parents died, and I moved into the orphanage. Sadie would climb in bed with me to calm me down during my first nights there because I couldn't stop crying for my mama."

Sadie smiled. "We don't remember it of course, but the matron who ran the orphanage told us when we were older. We were always best friends, but we had no idea why until it was explained."

"It's so good that you two have a bond that has lasted so long. It's good to have that kind of friendship. I have it with my younger brother."

"Yes, you'll meet him soon enough. Charles is nice enough, and at first I thought he'd be a good husband to you, but he's still a little too...wild doesn't seem to fit right, but it's all I can think of. He likes to have too much fun still. He wouldn't have been right for you." Grace set pancakes with bacon on the table in front of them.

"And you think Mr. Gabriel is right for me?" Sadie asked.

"I do think so. He's going to need some convincing though. He's agreed to marry you, but more than anything he needs a mother for his children. He's still in love with his late wife, Charlotte. His youngest is named after her as well."

Sadie bit her lip. "So I'm here to cook, clean, sew, and take care of children," she said. She loved the idea of being able to do those things, but she wished love came along with them.

"Don't you worry," Grace said. "He only thinks that's what he wants. He'll take one look at you, and he'll know that he really wants a wife."

Jack looked at his wife with a concerned look on his face. "Don't get her hopes up now. I have a feeling it's going to take longer than you think."

Grace said nothing else on the subject, but Sadie hoped her friend was right. The idea of living with a man who didn't want her around was a bit overwhelming.

After breakfast, Sadie helped with the dishes, and then she helped with the other chores. Grace kept telling her to sit, but Sadie had been sitting for so long, she felt like she never wanted to sit again.

"Can I scrub the floors for you?" Sadie asked. "I know that has to be hard in your condition."

"Near impossible!" Grace agreed. "But you're not here to do my cleaning. You're here to marry Mr. Gabriel."

Jack was no longer in the room, so Sadie felt comfortable asking, "When will I meet him?"

"He's going to come by with the children this evening. Thankfully, they've been with their grandmother today, or the girls' hair would look terrible. Mr. Gabriel tries so hard, but he has no idea what to do with a little girl's hair. I'm truly surprised he hasn't had it cut short like Steven's."

"Who is Steven?" Sadie asked.

"Oh, I forget you don't know them. The oldest is Rachel. She's six. Then comes Steven, who is four, and last is little Charlotte who is two. Charlotte and Rachel have the most beautiful golden hair."

"Oh, that's nice. His mother takes care of them during the day?"

"She does. You'll like Katie Bedwell. She's a very nice lady, and her children are all very well behaved. Stanley was her oldest, and from her first marriage, but he has siblings that are still in school. I believe she had four from her first marriage, married a widower with two boys, and then she had another six with Mr. Bedwell."

"That's what I've always wanted. A dozen children."

Grace laughed. "If anyone could convince you it's the perfect way to be, that person is Katie Bedwell. I'm hoping she comes by with Stanley and the children, but she may not. It depends on Mr. Bedwell, I'm sure."

"Does Mrs. Bedwell live near Mr. Gabriel?" Sadie asked, hoping fervently that her future mother-in-law would like her.

"Yes. They did the same thing that Jack did with his sister. They have adjoining properties, but they have their houses built right next to one another, and they farm the other sides. Not that his sister's husband is a farmer. He is a furniture maker. Every piece in this house was either made by him or by Jack who was trained by him."

"That's so nice!" Sadie said. "It makes everything feel more special and more comfortable, doesn't it?"

Grace nodded. "I couldn't love my little house any more than I already do. It's the house that Jack built."

Sadie smiled. "All right. I'm going to scrub these floors for you, while you rest a bit."

"I can't rest. I promised I would have cookies made up when Jack comes home for lunch. He has a sweet tooth. The man could eat more than our entire house ate back in Millshore."

"I'm sure you had to get used to cooking enough for a man like him. He seems like a good man."

"Oh, trust me, he is. Jack is everything I ever wanted in a husband and more. We're so excited about this baby. I even love his sisters. I promised Sarah we'd go over for tea this afternoon, and I'd take my cookies. Do you remember the cookies the matron at the orphanage taught us to make? It was one of our first baking lessons."

Sadie smiled, nodding. "I do remember. I loved those cookies, but I lost the receipt somewhere along the way."

"Those are the ones I'm making. If you want the receipt, I'll happily share." Grace stood with a mixing bowl cradled against her belly, and a wooden spoon in the other hand, mixing the cookie dough.

"Oh, that would be wonderful if you don't mind."

"When have I ever not shared something I had with you Sadie Rose Beckham?"

Sadie shrugged. She'd gotten her last name from the city the orphanage was in, because she'd been left there with no name or any kind of note. The matron had named her as she saw fit and that was that. "Never!"

"That's right. You have always been the sister I needed but that wasn't birthed by my mother. I guess we're sisters from different mothers."

"I know we are." Sadie smiled for a moment. "Should I change into my Sunday best to meet Stanley?"

"I would. You're not nervous about meeting him, are you?"

Sadie nodded. "How could I not be. He's going to accept me as a wife, but he doesn't want a wife. I feel like I'm infringing." She sighed. "I saved as much of his money as I could to give back to him. I hope he appreciates a frugal woman."

"You'd think all men would!" Grace told a quick story of how she'd been as thrifty as she could be when she'd first arrived, and how much it had upset Jack. "I have no idea why he didn't want me to use my own money for anything, but it's a big deal to him."

"Probably the male ego. I'm told men are too proud to let their women do anything."

"That might be the case. We really had problems with that when I first arrived." Grace set the bowl onto the worktable, and she started to drop the cookies. "I've been craving these, so thanks for coming and giving me an excuse to bake them."

"Have you had strange cravings?" Sadie asked, marveling at the wonders of pregnancy. Her friend was growing another person. It would never cease to amaze her that such things were possible.

Grace grinned sheepishly. "I have taken to mixing tomato sauce I've canned into my mashed potatoes."

"But...You don't like tomato sauce."

"I know!" Grace shook her head. "I suppose I've eaten many strange things while I've been carrying this child."

"Well, you look very healthy, and you're glowing. I'm so happy for you, Grace. I would ask for your happiness before mine any day, and I'm so happy you're doing well here."

For lunch they had simple sandwiches with what was left from Grace and Jack's roast beef the night before. Grace put a bit of gravy on everyone's for extra flavor, and as usual, Jack ate three sandwiches.

After lunch Sadie did the dishes while Grace put the cookies into a basket to take to Sarah's house.

"Sarah is Jack's older sister?" Sadie asked.

"Yes. When both their parents died on the trail, Sarah raised all three of her younger siblings. Can you imagine burying your parents and having to continue walking for another month or two?"

"I can't even imagine having parents!" Sadie said, grinning at her friend.

"I can't either. But it's nice to be part of a family now. Sarah has invited me into her world as if I was really her blood sister, and not just some girl who married her brother. I have to say I feel very comfortable around her and the entire Smith family." Grace smiled at Sadie. "I just know you're going to love them too."

"If you do, then you know I will." Sadie was surprised that she felt a bit of jealousy over Grace's happiness with the new family.

"Oh, Sadie, have I told you yet how happy I am that you're here? We may not be able to share a room or see each other every day like we did before, but at least we know we will see each other at least once or twice per week. I don't think you know how sad I was to leave you!"

"I understand completely. It was different for me. All the girls were gone. I mean, there were new girls, but it just wasn't the same. The poetry club died out, and I ended up using the time every week to write, but I so missed our friends meeting and talking about poetry as we did."

"I want to read something you've written lately!"

Sadie bit her lip, confessing her secret to the only person in the world who truly understood her. "I'm writing a book. I've done fifteen chapters so far."

"You have? Is it a romantic novel?"

"It is. I'll share it with you later. After tea but before Jack gets home. I couldn't share it with anyone else."

Chapter Three

Sadie greatly enjoyed tea and cookies with Sarah and Grace. The cookies were just as delicious as Sadie remembered—the only treat they'd really had at the orphanage. They brought back a great deal of memories and emotions.

After tea, they hurried home to Grace's house, and the two ladies made supper together. "Jack likes to have a lot of meat. He's not a fan of beans and thinks there should be meat with every single meal."

Sadie laughed. "I'm sure that gets expensive."

"It does, but he makes good money, and it makes him happy."

"I think that's what matters the most, isn't it?"

Grace smiled. "It is! He prefers beef, but tonight we're doing chicken and dumplings. He likes them almost as much as I do, and I make them often."

"Please tell me you use Mrs. Durant's receipt! Her chicken and dumplings inspire me to take on the world!"

"Of course, I do!"

Sadie found herself getting nervous. "What time is he supposed to be here?" she asked glancing at the clock.

"Oh, he's usually home by six for supper."

Sadie laughed. "Not Jack. Mr. Gabriel."

"Oh! Sorry. He said he'd be by around five. His mother makes all the family's meals now, and I know he wants you to take some of the chores from her. He feels as if he's taking advantage. Honestly, I think she does too. She really encouraged him to send for you."

"Do I look all right?" Sadie asked.

Grace looked up from the dumplings she was rolling out on the counter. "Stop worrying. You look beautiful just like always."

Sadie rolled her eyes. Grace had always tried to give her more confidence about her appearance, but to Sadie, Grace was the real beauty. "I hope he thinks so. Oh, Grace, give me something to do. I'm going to go crazy waiting for him."

"Calm yourself down, Sadie." Grace looked around for something her friend could do. "Here, start the chicken to boil, and then I need you to go out and collect the eggs. Now that I'm so far along, Jack insists that he be the one to do it, but he misses so many!"

Sadie smiled. "I will do my best to find every single egg." She quickly cut up and put the chicken, which had already been prepared, into the pot. They'd boil it for a good long while and pull it off its bones when it was completely cooked.

While they worked, Grace gave Sadie a rundown of the entire community. "Most families got here at the same time, having been on the Oregon Trail together, but others have joined here and there. Sometimes it's hard for a new person to be accepted into the community, and you can still see which families were the original settlers."

Sadie listened carefully as her friend told her of all the people in the town and which stores were available. "Do you have trouble with Indians here?" Sadie had read many tales about how the Indians attacked the people on the wagon trains. She half expected to see them in town, waving their tomahawks.

Grace shook her head. "We sometimes do some trading with them. Every week during the summer, they go to the north side of the lake to trade. We're always happy to get our hands on their fresh game. Then I salt it and preserve it for the winter. Winter seems to last at least six months here, but that's all right. It gives me an excuse to cuddle with Jack in front of the fire."

Sadie bit her lip, wanting to ask a question she could never ask anyone else. "Do you like that part of marriage, Grace? I've only heard women say it's a chore."

Grace blushed. "I don't consider it a chore, Sadie. If you love the man you're married to, it will seem very natural to want to be with him."

"Do you think Mr. Gabriel will want…"

"Not at first, I don't. I could be wrong though. He wants someone to help him with chores and children. He says he still loves his Charlotte too much to enter into another marriage."

Not for the first time, Sadie wondered what it would be like to be married to a stranger who was in love with someone else. She feared she'd made a mistake coming all this way to marry a man, sight unseen, but she wasn't in the factory. Certainly that made up for Mr. Gabriel's lack of interest in her.

Supper was almost ready when there was a knock on the door. Grace wiped her hands on her apron and went to the door, while Sadie watched. She was so nervous to meet the man, and she had no idea what she'd do if he thought she should get on a train and head straight back to Millshore.

Grace let a man into the house, followed by three children. Sadie stood watching from the kitchen, afraid to approach the man.

He watched her for a moment, then went to her in the kitchen. "I'm Stanley Gabriel."

As she looked at him, she realized he was a very handsome man. "I'm Sadie Beckham."

"It's nice to meet you." He held his hand out behind him, and the oldest child joined them. "This is my daughter, Rachel. The boy is Steven, and the little girl is Charlotte."

"It's nice to meet all of you."

Stanley studied her, as if he was wondering what was inside of her. "Do you like children?"

"I love them. I've always wanted a whole houseful."

"Well, I think I can offer you a good start on that." Little Charlotte came over and looked at Sadie, finally raising her arms and saying, "Up!"

Sadie picked up the little girl. "Hello!"

Charlotte put her first two fingers into her mouth and sucked on them, her huge blue eyes curious about the woman holding her.

"You have beautiful children," Sadie told Stanley.

He smiled. "I do at that. Almost as beautiful as their mother." He looked at Grace. "Is there a place I can speak with Miss Beckham privately?"

Grace smiled. "Yes, of course. And I have cookies and milk for the children."

"Thank you, Mrs. Smith."

Grace took the baby from Sadie, who led Mr. Gabriel into the parlor. She took a seat on one end of the sofa. "You're welcome to sit down." She felt like their whole interaction was so stilted.

Mr. Gabriel sat beside her on the sofa. "I don't know how much you know about my situation," he said.

"I know that your wife died two years ago, and that your mother has been helping you raise your three children. I know you need a mother for your children a great deal more than you want a wife."

He nodded. "All that is true. I don't want a wife at all. I plan for our marriage to be one in name only. That may change as the years go by, but I'm not certain it will. Basically, I'll be hiring you to be an unpaid, maid, cook, and mother to my children. Would such an arrangement work for you?"

She nodded. "I've always wanted to be a wife and mother. Hopefully our relationship will develop into more, but if it can't, I'm going into the marriage with open eyes."

"All right. Would a Saturday morning wedding be acceptable to you? Mrs. Smith told me she would like to keep you for a few days so you can catch up on all you've missed in one another's lives."

"Oh, yes. That's been going wonderfully. Marriage on Saturday morning sounds perfect."

"All right. I appreciate you understanding my feelings about my late wife. She passed unexpectedly when little Charlotte was born. She loved her babies more than anyone I know."

"And I'll love them too. Children need someone to care for them and nurture them to grow properly." Sadie gave a half smile, wondering how on earth she was going to be a good wife to a man who didn't care one whit for her.

They joined the children in the kitchen for milk and cookies, and Mr. Gabriel told them that Sadie would be their new mother. The children looked at her for a moment, but they didn't say anything against it. Apparently, they wanted a new mother.

After they'd left, Grace asked Sadie, "Well? What do you think of him?"

"I think he's very handsome, and there's a good chance that I'll fall in love with him, which would be a disaster." Sadie looked down at her hands, wondering if she should turn tale and run back to Beckham. It seemed as if it was the only prudent thing to do. But then she thought about the factory, and realized she needed to stay where she was. "Am I making a mistake?"

Grace took Sadie's hand in hers. "If I thought you marrying Stanley was a mistake, I wouldn't have sent for you. You know that."

"I know." Sadie looked at her hands. "The children seem well-behaved."

"Oh, they are. I've never heard a peep out of any of them at Sunday service."

"Well, that's good." Sadie took a deep breath. "Enough feeling sorry for myself. I want to be married, and he needs a wife, so I just need to bite the bullet and marry the man."

"Yes, you do." Grace smiled. "And if he makes you crazy, you come to me, and I'll set him straight!"

Sadie laughed. She could just picture pregnant Grace going up against a man the size of a lumberjack. "Do you think the baby gives you magical powers?" Sadie asked.

"If growing a baby isn't magical, I don't know what is."

Sadie sighed. "I hope he'll grow to at least like me. I mean, I'll be living in his house and all."

"Stop worrying! You're wearing the dress we made together for my wedding on Saturday. It's not like I can fit into it right now."

"You kind of look like you swallowed a watermelon seed, and it's harvest time!"

"I love you so much, I'm not going to hit you for saying that," Grace said, raising her chin. "I'm going to go finish supper."

"And I'm going to help!" Sadie wasn't about to be left behind.

Together the two women got supper on the table, and every time Sadie started to fret about her marriage, Grace convinced her it would all be all right. "But what if..."

"I'm not listening to one more what if, Sadie Rose! Set the table. You can't start being a laze about now."

"I suppose I can't." Sadie sighed dramatically. "I'll set the table." Sadie had no middle name, so Grace had started calling her Sadie Rose out of love for her.

When Jack came in at the end of the day, Sadie felt a little uncomfortable. It seemed strange that her friend was married and expecting a baby. It's what she'd wanted for both of them, but the fact it had actually happened was a bit frightening.

How had her life gotten so out of control? Sure, her shoulders didn't ache as much as they had, but she would have no real freedom as a wife. At the factory she'd been able to quit and move somewhere if she'd chosen. She'd be giving a man who was a relative stranger to her absolute power over all decisions in her life. It just didn't seem like the smart thing to do.

She was quiet through supper, feeling as if she shouldn't be there. Someday, she wanted to feel the love she could see between Jack and Grace, but it didn't seem to be in the cards for her.

After supper, she said, "Grace, spend time with your husband. I'll wash the dishes."

Grace looked like she wanted to protest, but Jack took her hand. "Thank you, Sadie. I will take my wife for a sunset walk."

Sadie cleared the table and started on the dishes as the couple went outside into the cool night air. She could hear them as they talked, but she tried not to listen. Instead, she worked on the novel she was writing in her head. Perhaps, she'd go to bed early and work on it there. She had a feeling it would be better if she left Grace and her husband alone.

Of course, that told her she had to marry Stanley. In the back of her mind she thought maybe she could stay with Grace and help with the baby, but Grace didn't need the interference in her marriage.

After the dishes were wiped and put away, she thought about going straight upstairs, but she needed to at least say goodnight to Grace and Jack. She found paper and a pencil to write with and she continued to write her novel, about a woman who went west to be a mail-order bride to a man who had lost his wife and had three young children. Art had to imitate life sometimes, didn't it?

She was deeply involved with her writing when the door opened and Grace and Jack came in. "I was hoping you'd still be up!" Grace said. "I want to read that novel of yours."

"Maybe it would be best to read it while Jack works. I don't want to interfere with your time with him."

Jack laughed. "No, you two have all of five days to spend together. You get Grace's time while you're here. I did appreciate you allowing me to borrow her for a walk."

Sadie frowned. "No, I couldn't do that!"

Jack smiled. "I get her every day for the rest of my life. Seriously, you two have fun with your book, and I'll go read my almanac. I want to see what the weather is supposed to be like this week."

Jack went into the parlor, while Grace sat down beside Sadie. "Are you writing a letter? Or working on your novel?"

Sadie smiled, a bit embarrassed. "I'm working on my novel. I can go and fetch what I've written so far, if you really want to read it."

"You know I want to read it!" Grace glared at Sadie. "You should have brought it downstairs while I was walking. Now I must wait."

Sadie laughed, taking the papers she'd written upstairs with her. It wouldn't be good for Grace to read it out of order, and she had known Grace long enough to know she wouldn't hesitate to peek.

Back downstairs, she handed Grace the pages she'd written, a little surprised at how thick the pages were. It was hard to believe she'd written all that. No wonder her hand ached, but it was a welcome change from her shoulders constantly aching.

While Grace read over what she'd written, Sadie continued writing. She loved listening to Grace's sighs and giggles as she'd read what she'd written so far. Perhaps when it was all written she could look back over it and be just as amused herself.

When Grace had read the last page and set it on the table, she turned to Sadie. "This had better have a happy ending!"

Sadie shrugged. "We'll have to wait and see, won't we?"

Chapter Four

By Saturday, Grace and Sadie were sad to see their time come to an end, but Grace was very excited about the wedding. Once Sadie was in Grace's dress, Grace had Sadie sit so she could fix her hair. "Do you remember how we used to always try out new hairstyles for each other back in the orphanage?" Grace asked.

Sadie laughed. "It's one of my fondest memories."

"Me too! I love how we would stay up late and try different hairstyles or add lace onto the hand-me-down dresses we were told to be grateful for." Grace shook her head. "Remember how hard it was to leave there and go work at the factory?"

Sadie nodded. "But we made wonderful friends in the boarding house!"

"I know, but the work was hard, and the hours were long. It's nice to be able to stand up straight again without all that shoulder pain."

"I agree." Sadie took a deep breath. "You need to tell me again I'm doing the right thing."

"I know it's hard to believe, but you are definitely doing the right thing! His mother will be so good to you, and she'll help you learn more about the children. I promise, you're doing the right thing!"

Sadie nodded and straightened her shoulders. "He's a good man, and he will be a good husband."

"That's right. Just keep thinking positively, and you'll do great."

"I'll do my best! And we'll have weekly tea on which day?"

"Let's do Wednesday afternoons at Sarah's. It'll be easier for me to take one baby than her to take the twins. And you can bring your two that aren't in school yet."

"How is Sarah going to feel about you volunteering her home for this?"

"She'll be thrilled. Sarah is very easy to get along with and goes along with just about everything."

Sadie stood and looked at her friend. "Do I look all right? I so wish I had blond hair."

"You're beautiful just the way you are," Grace said, hugging her friend.

"Only a best friend would say that and believe it!"

Sadie couldn't eat breakfast that morning as her stomach was twisted in knots. Instead, she went outside and sat on the front porch, in the rocking chair there. She rocked hard, trying not to think about how she was giving up all control over her life. For a man she loved, it would be worth it. For a virtual stranger? It didn't seem worth it at all.

A few minutes later they were driving to the church, and Sadie was praying. What else could she do but pray?

Mr. Gabriel was already at the church, his children in the pews with an older woman Sadie assumed was Mrs. Bedwell. Grace went to sit with Mrs. Bedwell, while Jack gave Sadie away. It seemed odd to have her best friend's husband give her away, but it wasn't like she could do anything else. She had no family other than Grace.

At the front of the church, Jack put her hand into Mr. Gabriel's, and she found herself looking at the man who would be her husband in a few short minutes. She listened to the pastor, and she must have said all the right things at the right times, though she couldn't remember doing so later.

When the pastor told Mr. Gabriel he could kiss his bride, he leaned down and brushed his lips against her cheek. Sadie wanted to cry at his reaction to kissing her, but she bit her lip and smiled at him. How could they ever fall in love if he wouldn't even kiss her?

She turned to see his youngest—Charlotte—sitting on Grace's lap and smiling. And that's when Sadie understood. She could fall in love with the children, and it would all work out just the way she needed it to. Focusing on the children and not on her husband's lack of love for her would make everything better.

Mr. Gabriel led her to Grace and the woman she assumed was his mother. "Ma, this is Sadie, the woman Grace has been hounding me to send for."

"Behave yourself, Stanley. This woman is getting you out of a real pickle, and you will be kind and loving. Understood?"

Sadie was surprised to see her new husband look ashamed. "Yes, Ma."

The woman turned her attention to Sadie. "It's so good to meet you. I've made a small snack for everyone so you can have a proper wedding reception."

Sadie smiled. "That sounds wonderful."

"Good, because it sounds good to me too. I want to help you get to know the children a bit."

Charlotte looked at Sadie and held her hands out. "Up!"

Sadie laughed. "I think this one and I are going to be just fine."

Charlotte stuck her first two fingers into her mouth again, just staring at Sadie.

Mrs. Bedwell smiled. "I do believe you're right. It's funny because she doesn't usually warm up to people quickly."

"Well, I can't wait to get to know all three children. Thank you for being willing to help me, Mrs. Bedwell."

"Oh, call me Katie. Everyone does." Katie stood and smiled. "Now let's go talk about these children and what they like to eat. And we'll get to know one another a little better."

As they started walking toward the back of the church, Mr. Gabriel said, "You two go ahead with the children. I need to get back to my harvest."

Katie stopped walking and glared at her son. "You will take today off from your harvest. Monday is soon enough."

"But, Ma!"

"Stanley Gabriel, you have just married this woman who came all the way across the country to be your wife and a mother to your children. You will spend this day with her. Is that understood?"

"I don't mind if Mr. Gabriel gets back to his harvest," Sadie said softly.

"He hasn't even asked you to call him by his given name? Well, you have my permission to do so. Stanley, get your wife's trunk out of the back of the Smith's wagon and put it in your own. You will treat her with every bit of the respect you showed Charlotte."

"Yes, Ma." Stanley was obviously past arguing with his mother. He wasn't going to win, and that was clear.

Once the trunk was moved, Stanley offered Sadie a hand to help her into the wagon. "Thank you," she said softly.

He nodded. "Everyone ready?" he asked.

Sadie held Charlotte, while Rachel stood up behind the seat. Steven sat quietly in the back. He had yet to say a single word to Sadie.

Stanley drove through the town and stopped at a house not too far out of town. "This is my ma's house. Mine is right over there." He pointed past a small line of trees to a large house not far from the one they were in front of. "My stepfather is a rancher, but I stuck to my pa's original plan when we came west, and I'm a farmer. I grow corn which ends up being fed to many of the ranchers' cattle in the area."

"Do you sell to your stepfather?"

"You bet I do. Sometimes I charge him double."

Sadie laughed at that. "Does that mean you don't get along with your stepfather?"

"Not at all. I love him. He got my ma out of a difficult situation, marrying her not long after my pa died. He also saved my younger sister from drowning in the North Platte River, almost dying in the process."

"That must have been frightening for everyone involved."

Stanley nodded. "The trail had already made Ma a widow. If she'd had a child taken from her as well, I don't know that she could have kept going." He set the brake and jumped down, walking around to help Sadie down. "Don't worry about acting all proper like. Ma isn't that kind of woman. She loves her kids and her grandkids, and she likes to have people over. She doesn't put on airs at all. You'll either love her or you won't."

"I think I will love her. I'm so thankful she has taken care of the children for long enough for me to arrive and take over." Sadie was going to love the children. Hopefully their pa would see that and fall for her because of it, but if he didn't, it wouldn't upset her too much. She refused to wait for him.

He took the baby from her and then helped her down from the wagon. "Go ahead in with Charlotte. I'll be right behind you with the other two."

Sadie nodded and went to the front door, knocking on it.

Katie opened the door. "Welcome! Come meet my husband." She led Sadie over to a grumpy looking man who was sitting at the table. "Katie, this is George. George this is our new daughter, Sadie."

George looked at her and smiled. "Nice to meet you." Then his face returned to the grumpy look she'd seen.

"Don't pay him no mind," Katie said. "I've been working with George on how to be kind to everyone around him. Sometimes he still forgets."

There seemed to be children everywhere, and little Charlotte started wriggling in Sadie's arms. After putting the child down, Sadie asked, "Is there anything I can help you with?"

"Not on your wedding day, there isn't!"

Grace came inside a short while later, Jack at her side. "Stanley isn't in yet?" Sadie asked, surprised.

"He's in the yard talking to the older two," Grace said. "How can I help, Katie?"

"Everything's ready," Katie replied. "Grab a plate and something to eat. We'll have cake if that son of mine ever comes inside."

Stanley chose that moment to open the door and come inside with his older two children. Rachel walked over to Sadie. "What should I call you?"

Sadie sat down in a chair so she would be eye-level with the girl. "My name is Sadie. You may call me that or whatever you wish. I will not insist you call me Ma."

"But what if someday I want to call you Ma?"

"Then you may. The choice is yours." Sadie had heard too many complaints in the orphanage about parents marrying and forcing their child to call the spouse Ma or Pa. The children always rebelled and many ended up in orphanages. She wouldn't do that to these children.

Rachel smiled. "I'll call you Sadie for now if that's all right."

"Absolutely. And I'll call you Rachel."

Rachel turned and skipped away, and Sadie saw that Steven had been lurking behind her. "How are you today, Steven?"

Steven shrugged and followed his sister.

Sadie looked at Katie. "Does he speak?"

"Not often. He talked nonstop until his mother died, and very rarely since. I hope he'll start talking more like he used to."

"It must have been hard on the older two to lose their mother that way."

Katie nodded. "Thankfully, I was nursing my youngest at the time, and I could just feed her. The infant food I've seen makes the babies sicker."

"I've heard goats' milk can be good. That's what we fed the babies at the orphanage. We just added a little bit of honey. Seemed to work. I'm sure it was fed to me because I arrived there as an infant."

Katie smiled. "Grace said the two of you met at the orphanage where you both grew up. I'm sure that was hard."

Sadie shrugged. "Maybe. I never knew anything different. I had Grace who I've always considered the sister of my heart. I think the one thing that was very difficult was that when we aged out of the orphanage at fourteen, we were sent to work at a factory, much before we were ready to be on our own. Thankfully, we went to the same factory, so we have always had each other."

"It must have been difficult for you when she came here to marry Jack."

"It was. Very difficult. We sent letters weekly, but it's just not the same as being able to speak in person." Sadie sighed. "It's nice to be able to see her again. It felt like forever."

"Well, I certainly hope you'll be happy with my Stanley. The children are well-behaved, and you can teach them so much about what they need to know. The girls both look so much like their mother, but little Steven looks just like his father did at that age. My late husband was Steven, and Stanley decided to name him after his pa."

George grunted. "He could have named the boy after me."

Katie frowned at George. "He has a right to honor his father."

George said nothing else. Katie shook her head at him, and he took it as an invitation to be silent.

Sadie did her best not to laugh. Katie seemed so sweet when they spoke, but she obviously had every man around her following her orders.

"What are the children's schedules?" Sadie asked, thinking it best to change the subject quickly.

Sadie was surprised when Stanley answered instead of his mother. "I wake them at five. We all dress and go to breakfast at Ma's at five thirty. Then I leave to go to work. Ma makes sure Rachel gets to school, and the two younger ones go down for a nap at one. I come at six for supper and take them home with me."

Sadie didn't even want to think about how empty his house would be of food. "Do we need to go for supplies so I can cook? Or do you have what we'll need?"

"I have no idea what you'll need. Maybe we should go to the store and leave the kids with Ma. I can introduce you to the shopkeeper and make sure he knows you can make purchases on my account."

Katie smiled. "You should pick up some fabric for new dresses for the girls as well. I give them the clothes my daughters have grown out of, but Charlotte has never had a new dress, and Rachel hasn't had one since her ma died. It would be a nice treat."

"And Steven?" Sadie asked.

"Steven doesn't care one whit what he wears. You could dress him in a flower sack, and he'd be happy. Be happier if you'd just let him run with nothing on, but we're trying to teach him that you don't take your clothes off just cuz you feel like it," Katie said. "You two go on and do the shopping. I'll mind the children. You might even want to take time to take her home and show her around without the children."

Stanley nodded. "Yes, Ma."

Chapter Five

After their shopping trip where she purchased all the staples a household should have, Stanley took Sadie back to his house. He helped her put everything away in the kitchen, and then invited her to see the rest of the house if she wanted to.

As she explored the house, she realized the girls shared a room, and Steven had his own room. There was no other room other than Stanley's. When she returned downstairs, she asked the question she was dreading the answer to. "Where will I sleep?"

He sighed. "I've been trying to figure that out. I think the only alternative is for you to share my room with me. The bed is big enough for two, and just because we're sleeping in the same bed, doesn't mean we need to be intimate."

"All right." Honestly, Sadie was both excited and nervous about the idea. If he was open to sharing his bed with her, whether they were intimate or not, then perhaps that was a future for them. She could only pray there was. "I think I got everything I need from the store including fabric for dresses for both of the girls."

"Good. They need new clothes, and my ma has her own little ones to take care of. She shouldn't be expected to do so much for my family. I hope you're willing to work hard to take the burden off her."

"Of course, I am. I wouldn't have agreed to the marriage otherwise. Is there anything you need me to focus on right away? Or should I just mind the children, clean, and deal with meals?" She'd noticed a thick layer of dust over almost everything in the house. None of the beds had been made either. She would teach the children how to help with those things.

"Ma put in a kitchen garden big enough for my family as well as hers. Would you be willing to help her harvest and get everything put up for winter?" Stanley asked, but he expected her to do it. It was written all over his face.

"Of course, I would. I really like your mother and can't wait to get to know her better."

He smiled and nodded. "She's been a blessing to me since Charlotte's death."

"I'm sure she has. I'm really glad she did so much to help out until I could get here." She looked around the kitchen once more, trying to think if there was anything else they needed from the store, but she couldn't think of anything. "I think we're set." There would just be a few days of cleaning to get the house in shape.

"Let's head back to Ma's. She's probably annoyed we left during the reception."

"There's no need for her to be. She told us to go!"

He shrugged. "I'll never be able to understand how her mind works."

When they returned to the gathering, most people had already gone, though Grace and Jack were still there. Sadie went to Grace and hugged her friend. "You probably need to get home. I worry about you doing so much."

Grace laughed. "How can going to a wedding and a reception be too much? Now I don't have to cook the noon meal!"

Sadie smiled, thinking of the cleaning and baking that needed to be done at her new home. There was so much to do, and she was both dreading all the work, and looking forward to it. What a blessing to be able to work for her family and not for the small amount she made at the mill.

Little Charlotte was in one corner of the room by herself, looking as if she was about to fall asleep. Sadie looked at Stanley. "I think it's time to get the children home for a nap. Don't you?"

He nodded. "You carry Charlotte, and I'll go find Steven."

Sadie went to Katie. "Thank you so much for the reception and for taking care of the children while we were at the store. It is very much appreciated. We're going to take the children home to nap now."

Katie stood and embraced her new daughter-in-law. "Don't worry. I'll still be helping as needed."

"Let me know when you're ready to harvest and put-up food for the winter. I plan to help."

Katie smiled. "I would welcome the help! I like the gardening, but canning is not my favorite."

"Looks like I got here just in time then. I haven't done any canning since I was in the orphanage, but I remember how, and would love to help."

"Thank you!"

They walked home with the children, having left the wagon in front of their own home instead of Katie's. Carrying Charlotte made Sadie's heart soar. She was not heavy, and the way she wrapped her little arms around her neck was such a good feeling.

Once the children were down for their naps, Sadie made her way into the kitchen to start supper. She decided to make a pot roast with potatoes and carrots, something that was simple, yet very filling.

After peeling the potatoes and carrots, she added them to a large pot with the roast and put it into the oven. Then she scrubbed the worktable and started baking bread to go with their supper.

Stanley had left saying he'd be home at six for supper, and Sadie had the kitchen to herself until Rachel joined her. "Can I help?"

Sadie smiled at Rachel and nodded. "Of course." There was a child sized apron hanging from a hook on the wall, and Sadie took it down and tied it for Rachel. "I'm baking bread, making supper, and getting the kitchen clean. Supper is in the oven now, but you could help with the bread, or you could help with the cleaning."

Rachel seemed to consider for a moment. "I'll help with the cleaning, but may I punch down the dough when it's time?"

"Yes, you may," Sadie said. "I'm going to sweep the kitchen floor. Would you like to hold the dustpan for me?"

Rachel nodded emphatically. "I do this for Granny sometimes."

Sadie had a hard time thinking of Katie as a granny. She was still young and full of life. "Well, I'm glad you already know how. I'm sure Granny has taught you a lot, hasn't she?"

"My ma died, and she was the only one to teach me after that. Granny loves us, but I think we make her tired sometimes."

"I'm sorry your ma died."

Rachel nodded. "Me too. Sometimes I close my eyes and think about her, but I can't remember what she looked like. I should remember, shouldn't I?"

"You were only four when she passed. How could you remember her?"

"I remember she read to me at night, and she always tucked me in. And I remember I couldn't fit on her lap cuz Charlotte was so big."

Sadie smiled. "That's more than I remember about my ma. You should write down everything you remember about her, so you will always remember those things."

"Would you help me?" Rachel didn't seem to know if she should like Sadie or be afraid of her.

"I would love to help."

"You're not a real stepmother at all!" Rachel said,

"What do you mean?" Sadie asked.

"Well, Cinderella had a stepmother, and she made her do all the chores and was mean to her."

Sadie smiled. "Who read the story of Cinderella to you?"

"Granny. And Ma."

"Well, I'm still a stepmother, just not a wicked one."

Rachel nodded. "I'm glad you're not wicked. Pa wouldn't be happy with you if you were."

"I'm sure he wouldn't. He loves you children too much for that." Sadie finished the sweeping and washed her hands before peeking at the bread. "It's ready to punch down."

Rachel clapped. "It's my favorite part of baking bread!" She waited as Sadie brought the dough to the table for her, washing her hands while she did. Then she stood on a chair and used her fists to punch down the dough.

Sadie laughed. "You're really punching it!"

"I'm strong too!" Rachel said, her little hands flying as they attacked the dough.

"I can see that!" Sadie said. "Do you want to knead it, or do you want me to do that part."

"I'm not strong enough to knead it yet. Granny said so."

"Well, you're not going to get strong enough to do it unless you try!" Sadie took the dough out and put it on the table she'd floured. She broke off a small chunk of the dough. "There, you knead that part of it."

Rachel's eyes were wide. "Really?"

"Of course!"

Together, they kneaded the dough and put it into greased pans so it could rise again. Rachel found a towel and carefully draped it over the three pans of bread dough. "There. Now it will rise."

"Yes, it will. And while it's rising, I need to scrub the kitchen floor. It doesn't look like it's been done for a while."

Rachel shook her head. "Pa's too tired after work to clean house. And he said Granny couldn't do it because there was too much to do, taking care of two families like she was. I guess the floor has been waiting for you."

"I guess it has." Sadie took the water she'd been boiling and added a bit of soap to it. She found a scrub brush and went to a corner of the room, getting down on her hands and knees.

"I can't help?" Rachel looked like she was close to tears.

"I only saw one scrub brush. I'm sorry."

"I know where another one is!" Rachel hurried away and came back with a smaller scrub brush.

Sadie smiled. "Now you can help."

Stanley chose that moment to go back into the house for a glass of water. He looked at the two of them, the blond head close to the brunette. Both of them were scrubbing as if making the floor clean was the only thing that mattered in the world. Perhaps she wasn't the woman he'd have chosen for a wife, but it looks like he made the right choice for the mother of his children.

"That floor is starting to look spotless," he said.

Rachel turned to him, and he could see the pure joy on her face. "I'm helping Sadie. And she let me punch down the bread and hold the dustpan. She doesn't think I'm underfoot at all."

"You've always been a good worker, Rachel." Somehow, just having Sadie in his home made him feel like some of the weight of the world that had been on his shoulders for the past two years had dissipated some.

Sadie never even glanced his way as she said, "Rachel is a good helper. I'm glad to have someone like her."

For a moment, Stanley felt a pang. The woman was his wife, and she didn't even look at him? What was wrong? He didn't want a real marriage, but he realized he wanted her to want a real marriage. Even his thoughts made no sense at all.

"You two keep going. I can already see a difference." Stanley went back outside to work, but his mind was on the two heads scrubbing together on his kitchen floor. Sadie was obviously willing to teach his children as much as she could.

When the floor was finally finished, it was time to put the bread in the oven. Sadie washed her hands again, knowing the kitchen floor would need a couple more good scrubbings before it was to her standards of cleanliness.

After popping the bread into the oven, she dramatically wiped her brow with the back of her hand. "We've worked hard!"

Rachel nodded. "We should go check on Charlotte. Sometimes she wakes up scared."

"I don't hear her crying."

"We should check," Rachel said again.

"All right. Let's go." Sadie wasn't sure why they were going, but Rachel obviously thought it was very important.

When they reached the top of the stairs, Sadie heard jabbering. She walked to the girls' room and looked inside to see Charlotte sitting in her bed playing with her toes. "I thought you were sleeping!" Sadie said, laughing as she pulled the child from her bed.

"Granny always takes her right to the outhouse when she wakes up. She's just learning how to go in there," Rachel said.

"Let's check on your brother."

Rachel led the way to Steven's room, opening the door. Steven was standing in the middle of his room, wearing nothing more than a smile. "What happened to your clothes?" Sadie asked, unable to keep the grin from her face.

He pointed to a corner of the room, and sure enough, there was a small pile of clothes there. She wondered if she should do the laundry on Sunday. She didn't like to break the Sabbath, but she knew they all needed clean clothes.

It seemed that Katie had done a great deal for the family, but not quite enough at the same time.

"We're going to the outhouse, Steven. Do you want to come with us?"

Steven nodded, heading for the door.

"No, Steven, if you're going with us, you have to put some pants on."

Steven shrugged and sat down on the floor in his room. He was obviously not willing to go if he had to wear anything.

Sadie decided not to worry about it as they went downstairs and outside to the outhouse. Charlotte pulled down her bloomers and sat down. "I did it!"

Sadie smiled. "You sure did! What a good girl you are." All at once, Sadie knew marrying Stanley had been the right decision. She barely knew these children and already she loved each of them.

As they headed back toward the house, Sadie wondered if Steven would keep his clothes on if she let him wear his night shirt all day. He obviously didn't like the constriction of real clothes, but would he complain if he was mostly free?

She'd have to bring it up to Stanley later.

When they got back into the house, she could smell the bread baking and stopped to sniff deeply. "Oh, how I love the smell of fresh-baked bread. Don't you?"

Rachel said, "It's my favorite thing!"

"Well, let's go peek at it and see if it's done."

"I'll hold onto Charlotte, so she doesn't touch the stove."

Sadie frowned at the little girl. "Does she do that?"

"No, but I always hold her when the stove is going, so she might."

"Charlotte, the stove is very hot. You don't want to get burned, do you?"

Charlotte shook her head, her blonde curls bouncing.

"Then you never touch the stove. All right?"

Sadie put the little girl down into a kitchen chair as she opened the oven, using her apron as a potholder. "It looks like it's almost ready," Sadie said. "I bought some butter at the store today, but we'll start churning our own this week. Have you ever made butter?"

Rachel shook her head. "I can't wait to learn how!"

Chapter Six

When Stanley walked into the house at just before six, he could see all the work that had been done since the wedding earlier. The house smelled of fresh-baked bread and something else he couldn't quite place.

The children were all clean and for some reason Steven was wearing his nightgown, but at least he was wearing something. The boy usually was naked the minute they got into the house.

Rachel was setting the table and looked like she was happier than she'd been in a long time. Charlotte was clean and sitting at the table with a piece of bread in her hand that she was gobbling up.

"Is the bread good, Charlotte?" he asked.

Charlotte nodded and said something, but he couldn't understand because her mouth was too full of bread.

Sadie came into the dining room from the kitchen with a bowl that she set on the table, and then she turned around and went right back. So far, his choice of bride was exactly what he needed. She was good with children. She cleaned and her cooking smelled like it was phenomenal.

She came back in with a platter that was filled with pot roast. His mouth watered just looking at it. When she turned back to the kitchen, Rachel followed her as if she'd been following the woman her entire life. Rachel came back with a plate with a ball of butter on it, and Sadie brought a bowl of gravy. He stared at the food and decided he needed to wash his hands. He was too hungry to care about anything else.

When he returned, they were all sitting at the table, just waiting for him. "Would you say grace?" Sadie asked.

For the first time in a long time, Stanley was feeling thankful. In his prayer he thanked God for sending Sadie to them. Perhaps she wasn't blonde like Charlotte had been, but she was a blessing straight from heaven. He could see it now and wondered why it had taken him so long.

They passed the food in an orderly fashion. Sadie showed each child what she wanted them to do, and they did it. Stanley couldn't help but be impressed, and he hadn't even tasted the food yet.

When all their plates were fixed, he took a bite of the potatoes and gravy. "This is delicious! Why were you working in a mill and not as a cook?"

Sadie smiled. "I'm so pleased you like it. I have many receipts for things I've enjoyed over the years. I'll learn from your mother as well."

Stanley shook his head. "You're much better than my mother. I'd rather you didn't learn from her."

Sadie laughed, thinking he was joking, but his face was completely serious. "I thought the food your mother made for the reception was very good."

"Yes, it was. She's very good, but you far surpass her."

Rachel took a bite of the meat and said, "You really are a good cook, Sadie. I'm glad you're my new ma and will teach me to cook like you do."

Stanley felt a pang at Rachel's words. Were the children warming up to their new stepmother too quickly?

Throughout the meal, they got to know one another's tastes in food. After a few questions, Sadie had a better idea of what she should cook.

"I have a question for you," Sadie said.

"What's that?"

"I tried asking Steven, but he hasn't spoken in front of me yet. I'm wondering if you would mind if I kept him in a nightshirt during the day? He's not taking it off as quickly."

Stanley pursed his lips, thinking about it. He didn't know what it would hurt to let the boy wear nightshirts. "I want him to wear pants if we're leaving the house, but I don't mind if he wears a nightshirt when he's home."

Sadie looked at Steven. "Will you keep the nightshirts on and wear pants when we leave the house?"

Steven nodded, his hair flopping.

"Looks like I need to give you a haircut," Sadie said.

"I could use one too," Stanley told her. "If you don't mind that is."

"There's no barber in town?"

He shook his head. "No, not yet. Remember this whole town is only about sixteen years old."

"I'll happily cut your hair then. I can't promise it will be perfect, though. I've never done it before."

Stanley shrugged. "Doesn't make much difference to me."

After the meal, Sadie started to clear the table and realized Rachel was right beside her helping. "You certainly are going to make some man a good wife one day," Sadie said.

Stanley couldn't help but smile. Sadie complimented the children and made them feel like they were worth something. Even their own mother hadn't excelled at that.

Stanley took Steven and Charlotte into the parlor with him while Sadie and Rachel did the dishes. Steven seemed much happier than usual. "Do you like Sadie?" Stanley asked.

Steven nodded emphatically.

"And you like wearing your nightshirt during the day?"

This time Steven treated Stanley to one of his rare speeches. "It doesn't make my thing hurt."

Stanley blinked a couple of times. "Pants make your thing hurt?"

Steven nodded.

Stanley wasn't sure why his son had that problem, but he decided it would be best not to explore too much.

When Rachel and Sadie joined them a short while later, Rachel was clutching a notebook to her chest. "Sadie said she'd help me," Rachel said.

Stanley watched as Rachel and Sadie sat together on one end of the sofa. "What is she helping you with?"

"I want to write down all my memories of Ma, so I won't forget them when I'm older."

Stanley wanted to get up and leave the room, rather than watch the two of them work together on something about Charlotte. "Why?"

Sadie looked at Stanley. "Rachel only has a few memories of her mother. She wants to be able to write everything she remembers down now, so she can refer to those memories later. It's a way of keeping her mother alive for her."

He didn't know why it bothered him so much, but it did. Sadie shouldn't be talking to Rachel about Charlotte. It wasn't her place. Her place was to see that the children were happy. That was all.

The two of them worked together with Sadie spelling words that Rachel was unfamiliar with. Since Rachel had just started school the previous month, there was little she knew how to spell on her own.

When they were finished, Rachel took her notebook upstairs.

Stanley decided not to say anything about it. He'd wait until they were alone and explain how he felt about her getting involved with his children's memories of their mother.

The family sat together, Stanley reading from the Farmer's Almanac, and Sadie talked with Rachel while the younger two played on the floor with some blocks.

When it was dark, Sadie stood up. "It's time for bed."

Stanley watched her, wondering how she'd deal with bedtime. He always had a hard time getting the children to go to bed, but she seemed ready to deal with everything.

After they'd all made a trip to the outhouse, Sadie ushered the children upstairs, promising them a story. He followed along to see how she did with them.

All three children snuggled together onto Rachel's bed, while Sadie told them of a little girl who didn't have any parents at all and lived in an orphanage. The story culminated when another little girl came to the orphanage, and the two became best friends for all their lives.

Rachel smiled. "Do you know the little girl?"

Sadie nodded. "Want to know a secret?" At Rachel's nod, she continued. "I'm the little girl. And Mrs. Smith? She's the little girl who moved to the house later. And we've been best friends all our lives."

Rachel smiled. "I want to have a best friend like that."

"I do hope you will. Having a best friend is having someone to always share your secrets with. Who will be there for you when you fall down and when you need a shoulder to cry on, or someone to be silly with. Best friends are better than anything!"

"I'll pray for a best friend just like Mrs. Smith."

Sadie tucked each girl under her covers, and kissed their foreheads, telling them goodnight. And then she followed Steven and did the same. "Sleep sweet, little man," she said softly.

When she closed Steven's door and there was no begging for another story or a glass of water, Stanley realized she had his children under some sort of spell. "Are you a witch?" he asked.

Sadie frowned at him. "That's not a nice thing to ask."

"Well, you have put some sort of spell on my children. They're not even protesting bedtime."

She laughed, understanding then. "They're sweet children. I'm going to be very happy to be a part of their lives."

Stanley shook his head. "I put your trunk into our room. I'll give you ten minutes to get ready for bed, and then I'll join you."

Sadie nodded. "All right." She'd change quickly and be in bed by the time he returned. She had no desire for the man to see her in her nightgown, or even worse, without it.

She changed quickly and took her hair down, brushing through it to get any tangles out. Then she slipped under the covers, hoping the side she'd chosen to sleep on would be satisfactory.

She lay there for a minute or two before he knocked on the door and let himself in. He turned the lamp down and undressed in the dark. She heard the sounds of his clothing falling to the floor.

When he moved to get under the covers, she felt the bed dip, and then he settled on the pillow beside hers. It felt so strange being in bed with a man who was her husband, who had never even kissed her properly.

"Goodnight, Sadie," he said.

"Goodnight," she whispered back.

She lay awake long after she heard his soft snores that told her he was asleep. She prayed that things would change between them. She was already in love with his children. Surely, she'd be in love with him soon as well, whether she wanted to be or not.

When Sadie woke the next morning, she realized she was completely pressed up against Stanley, and he was hugging her back to his front. She could tell by the pre-dawn light it was time for her to get up and start breakfast.

She tried to pull away from her husband to get out of bed, but he clamped his arm around her even tighter. Slowly, she edged out from under the arm, and dressed in the dark before rushing downstairs to start the first meal of the day.

As she tiptoed out of the room, Stanley lay with his eyes open watching her. She'd woken him with her struggles to get out of bed, and he felt as if he'd betrayed Charlotte's memory by moving so close to her in bed.

He vowed he would do better the next night. He didn't need to hold her as he had simply because she was a warm female body in his bed. He had to keep up the mental wall between them. There was no other option.

Sadie decided to make eggs and bacon with toast for breakfast. She heard Stanley come downstairs as she was cutting the strips of bacon, but she didn't look at him. She was certain she wouldn't be able to meet his eyes.

"Doing morning chores," Stanley said as he went out. Perhaps he was as uncomfortable with the way they'd woken up as she was.

She had just finished buttering the toast and putting it into the oven when Rachel came downstairs holding her sister's hand. "How can I help, Sadie?"

Having anticipated just such a question, Sadie said, "I have the eggs broken into a bowl. Can you break the yolks and stir them, so I can turn them into scrambled eggs?"

Rachel had Charlotte sit at the table while she did as she was asked. "This is fun!"

Sadie smiled. "I enjoy cooking so much. I'm hoping you will too."

"I know I will." Rachel finished with the eggs and watched as Sadie fried up the bacon and set it on a plate. "Now the eggs?" she asked.

"Yes. And the toast is in the oven." Sadie added the eggs to the bacon grease. "Do you want to set the table for us?"

"Yes!" Rachel carried the dishes to the dining room, setting the table for the family.

When everything was done, Sadie carried the food into the dining room and set it on the table. She poured two cups of coffee but waited for Stanley to return before pouring glasses of milk for the children.

She still couldn't meet his eyes, but it seemed that he wasn't meeting hers either. Odd. Could it be that he was as embarrassed as she was? And if so, how could they get past it?

They were married and planned to wake up together every day for the next sixty years or so. They couldn't avoid talking to each other or looking at each other for that long.

She set the milk on the table and realized that Steven hadn't come down for breakfast yet. And they had church in just a couple of hours.

Rachel noticed her brother was missing as well. "I'll go find Steven."

Before Sadie could respond, the girl was flying up the stairs to fetch her brother, so they could all have breakfast. "I don't know what you like to eat for breakfast, so I made eggs, bacon, and toast. Would you prefer oatmeal or something like that?" Sadie was proud of how calm she sounded as she asked.

Stanley shrugged. "This is good. I like pancakes and johnny cakes as well."

"All right. What about fried potatoes?"

"Just as good," he said. "I'm really not picky."

"Good. That'll make everything easier, won't it?"

He nodded as Rachel hurried into the dining room with Steven. "He was still sleeping!" Rachel said, shaking her head at her brother.

At least he wasn't naked, Sadie though.

After a quick prayer, they dug into the meal. Sadie didn't feel up to making conversation, so she was glad when Rachel chattered on about how much she loved Pastor Jed and his wife.

Stanley didn't seem to have anything to say either. Sadie couldn't help but wonder if he was going to find a way to change their sleeping arrangements.

Chapter Seven

Sadie found church enjoyable, even though she still couldn't look at her husband. Katie took her and Charlotte around and introduced her to many different people.

Grace walked with them, telling her little stories she knew about everyone from time to time. The pastor was kind and spoke about marital love and being faithful. It was strange to her because she had never met a pastor who was so welcoming and open with his congregation.

After church, Katie invited their family to Sunday dinner, and Sadie graciously accepted.

At the Bedwell house, they all had a thick stew made with beef, carrots and potatoes, and Sadie enjoyed it immensely. "This is very good!" Sadie said. "I want the receipt when you have a little time."

"Of course, I'd be happy to share it with you." Katie wrote down the receipt as soon as they were finished with the meal.

When Katie spotted Steven a short while later, while she and Sadie were cleaning up, he was naked as usual. "I let him wear his nightshirt all day yesterday, and he never took it off. He doesn't like pants."

Katie shook her head. "That boy marches to the beat of his own drummer. I think he may have an entire band in his head, telling him exactly what to say and do."

"So he does talk?" Sadie had yet to hear the boy say a word.

Katie nodded. "He does. He simply prefers not to. But if you give him some blocks, the things he makes are amazing."

Sadie had known a boy much like Steven in the orphanage. She had no intention of trying to make the boy speak. "Rachel has been very enthusiastic about helping with chores around the house. Is that normal for her?"

Katie smiled. "Sometimes. She really enjoys helping to cook and bake."

"She helped me bake bread yesterday, and she even got down on her knees with a scrub brush and helped me clean the kitchen floor. I kept expecting her to get bored and go do something else, but she stayed and worked with me until it was done."

"That's not what she usually does, but I think she's very excited to have a mother again. She was lost for a while after Charlotte died."

"Charlotte must have been very special," Sadie said.

Katie shrugged. "Not so much. She and Stanley fell in love at school, and they married when they were twenty-one. She was always very sweet when Stanley was around, but she never offered to help with dishes or anything like that. For a while it seemed she was going to keep the children from me, but that never happened."

"Stanley speaks of her as if she was a goddess or something."

"To Stanley, she was. Not to anyone else. Her folks moved back east after she and Stanley married, and Charlotte begged to follow. Stanley came here to farm, though, and he couldn't have afforded a farm back east."

"Sounds like she was a bit difficult."

Katie shrugged. "To be honest, you and I have had more in-depth conversations already than Charlotte and I ever did."

"Well, I hope you don't mind me asking for parenting advice when it's needed." Sadie couldn't imagine why Stanley was so enamored of a woman who had been less than kind to his mother. It simply didn't make sense to her.

"Not at all. I would adore it. I always wanted a good relationship with Charlotte, but she didn't care to have one with me."

After the dishes were finished, Sadie gathered the children, and they went home. Stanley was already back out in the fields working, breaking the Sabbath. He said the crops needed to be harvested soon. All the corn was up, but he was also digging potatoes. He'd said something about doing half and half that year, so she left him to it.

She and Rachel put Steven and Charlotte down for their naps, and Steven was thrilled to put on his nightshirt. Sadie had no idea why he hated pants so very much, but he did, and they would just have to work with him on it.

Rachel followed Sadie back to the kitchen. "What are we making for supper?" she asked.

"How about chicken and dumplings?" Sadie asked. "It's one of my very favorite meals."

Rachel frowned. "I don't think I've ever had it."

"You're in for a treat then!" Sadie had already plucked the feathers from a chicken Stanley had butchered that morning after breakfast. "We're going to boil the chicken, and then we'll make the dumplings after we take the chicken off the bones."

Rachel nodded. "Just tell me what to do."

Sadie smiled at the girl. "You don't have to help if you don't want to."

"I do want to!"

"All right, let's get started then." Sadie cut the chicken into pieces, and put it into a huge pot of water before putting it on the stove. "It'll take hours for the chicken to be just right, but I like to put a little seasoning in."

While Rachel watched, Sadie washed her hands. She hated touching raw meat, but there was really no other way to cook. Then they went into the dining room and Sadie said, "I think we should wash windows today. How does that sound?"

Rachel nodded emphatically. So the two of them set to work, washing all the windows. When they were done, Sadie thanked Rachel for being such a big helper.

"Tomorrow, I have to do laundry."

Rachel pouted. "I want to help with laundry, but I have school tomorrow."

"Why don't I get it all washed and on the clothesline, but when you get home, you can help me get it off the line and folded and ironed?"

Rachel nodded. "I like that idea!"

"Good. Do you walk to school? Or do you get a ride?"

Rachel shrugged. "When it's raining Pa drives me, but mostly I walk. He said when it's really cold this winter, he'll give me rides too."

"I think that's very smart. You don't want to get frostbite."

"Granny always says that too!"

Sadie laughed. "I have a feeling there are lots of things that both your granny and I say. Don't you think?"

"I think so." Rachel smiled. "What do we do now?"

"Let's dust all the furniture. The floors in the whole house need to be scrubbed too. There's a lot to be done around here."

"I can help with the floors!" Rachel said excitedly.

"All right, then we'll sweep and scrub the floors today."

The two of them went to fetch the broom and dustpan, and Rachel carefully held the dustpan while Sadie swept into it. Sadie decided to start with the parlor because it was a smaller room than the dining room. Once the floor was scrubbed in the parlor, she said, "Let's go check on our chicken."

Together they went to the kitchen and washed their hands in the basin. "Now we have to take the chicken from the broth and take it off the bone. I'll put all the chicken into a big bowl, and we'll get the skin and bones off of it. It'll be hot so you're going to need to be careful."

Together, they used forks and knives and got the chicken off the bone and back into the pot. "Now, we need to mix the dumplings. This is the fun part," Sadie said.

Rachel giggled as they got dough all over their hands making the dumplings. When it was time to drop them into the pot with the chicken and broth, Sadie had her step back. "It's going to splash some, but I don't want it to splash you."

"I think Charlotte is awake. I can hear her," Rachel said.

"Do you want to go get her and take her to the outhouse while I put the dumplings in?"

"I can do that!"

As soon as she'd finished with the dumplings, Sadie went upstairs to find Steven. He was sitting on the floor in his nightshirt, stacking blocks. He put them into perfectly neat rows, and then stacked them atop one another.

"Let's go use the outhouse, Steven."

Steven frowned.

"You can play with your blocks after supper," Sadie promised.

Steven reluctantly got to his feet and went with Sadie to the outhouse.

When that chore was finished, Sadie washed her hands and went to check on the dumplings. They didn't take long.

She found a slotted spoon and took one dumpling from the bubbling pot, putting it in a bowl. After tasting it, she realized it was done. Glancing at the clock, she saw that it was just before six. Rachel set the table, while she put the food on. She'd made enough for lunch the following day as well.

At five minutes past six, Stanley came in, his hands and arms covered with mud. "Supper's ready," Sadie told him, forgetting not to look him in the face. After she did, she immediately looked away.

He went to the basin and washed his hands before joining them at the table. After the prayer, he asked, "What did you get up to this afternoon?"

Rachel answered. "Sadie and I made supper, and we washed the windows and scrubbed the floor in the parlor. It's clean now!"

"Seems to me that more and more of the house is getting clean every day."

"Sadie and I want it clean so we work on it together."

Stanley looked at the food in his bowl. "What's this?" he asked.

"Chicken and dumplings," Sadie told him. "One of my very favorite meals, so I hope everyone else likes it too."

He took a bite, and nodded, smiling. "Very good. You can make this every week."

She smiled. "I'd love to!"

The children liked the meal as well, and she made a mental note to make it often. Learning the tastes of a whole family at once was proving to be much easier than she thought it would be.

Charlotte ended up wearing the meal. It was even in her hair, so Sadie knew there would be some child bathing happening soon. She had yet to see a bathtub there. "Where's the bathtub?" she asked. "I'm going to need to get Charlotte clean soon."

"In the cellar, up against the back wall." Stanley frowned. "Do you need me to bring it up for you?"

"I can manage." Sadie knew that she'd bathe the following afternoon while he worked, and the children napped. "What time does Rachel go to school?"

"She needs to be there by nine. She usually walks, and it takes her a half hour to get there. Just have her leave by quarter after eight, and she'll have time to play before school starts."

"I need to get some fabric to make a couple more nightshirts for Steven. If that's all he's going to wear, he's going to be getting them terribly dirty. I assume he only has one?"

Stanley nodded. "Never occurred to me he'd need more than one."

"Should I wait until you can take me to the store? Or should I walk with the children?"

"Wait. Or tell me what fabric you need, and I'll pick it up for you."

"I'll make it out of calico. What color do you want, Steven?"

To her surprise, he answered her. "Red."

Sadie looked at Stanley. "We need red calico."

"How much?"

She shrugged, looking at Steven. "Get four yards. I should be able to make two or three out of that."

"All right. I'll go in the morning. Do you want a ride to school then, Rachel?"

Rachel nodded. "I like it when you take me to school, Pa."

"You don't like to walk?" Sadie asked.

"I don't mind walking, but I get Pa all to myself when he takes me to school."

Sadie hadn't considered that. Stanley had been her only parent for two years, and she got little time with him. "Then you should ride with your pa."

"I'll come straight home after school to help with the laundry," Rachel promised.

"All right. We'll have lots of fun taking it off the line and folding it." Sadie hated laundry, but if Rachel was excited to do it, she'd not make her feel like it was a dreaded chore. She looked at Stanley. "I was told there's a quilting circle on Wednesday afternoons. Do you mind if I go?"

He shook his head. "You'll probably have to swap out weeks with Ma. She'll be thrilled to get to go half the time."

"I guess she hasn't been able to do much during the day since she's been watching the little ones, and she has her own young ones."

He nodded. "Her youngest is Steven's age. They get along pretty well."

"A boy or girl?" She couldn't believe she couldn't remember. She'd had Sunday dinner with the family just hours before.

"Boy. They seem more like siblings than uncle and nephew."

"I can see that. I'm glad Steven has a playmate his age."

"I am too. Nate loves it when Steven comes over. I'm sure you'll be watching him while Ma takes her turn going to the quilting circle."

"Where is the quilting circle?"

"At the church. There's a big room that's used for church socials and anything else people want to use it for. So it's the perfect place for the quilting circle."

"Do you know if women ever take their children along?"

Stanley shrugged. "No clue. You'll have to ask Ma."

"All right, I will. Is there a butcher shop in town?" she asked.

He nodded. "Next door to the mercantile. Do we need meat for supper tomorrow?"

"I could make beans if you prefer, but I get the feeling you prefer meat." Sadie had grown up only eating meat once per week. It didn't seem to be that way in this little town.

"I do prefer meat with every meal. Beans every once in a while are all right, but we ate so many beans on the trail, I doubt if anyone in this town will eat beans often."

"That makes sense. Beans would have stored well in the back of the wagon."

He nodded. "We got to the point we'd beg Ma not to make us eat beans. I don't think she's made them since we settled."

"I don't blame her. She's probably sick of them as well."

"I think George told her if she ever fixed beans again, he'd toss them out the window. He's a much nicer man since Ma married him, but he's still grumpy more often than not."

"He wasn't nice before?"

Stanley shook his head. "No one liked him before he and Ma started courting. After, they tolerated him. He never beat us though. I guess that means he was a good pa."

Sadie sighed. "I guess so."

Chapter Eight

By the time Sadie and Stanley had been married a month, they had found each other's rhythm, and getting into bed with each other every night was getting easier for them both.

Stanley was still very standoffish when he was awake, but during the night, he always ended up snuggled against her. She could say it was the cold, but it was unseasonably warm.

She woke up in the middle of the night, and he was kissing her, and not just a peck on the lips. His hands were all over her, one pushing the bottom of her nightgown up a little.

She knew she should pull away and remind him who she was, but it felt nice, and she just couldn't seem to say anything. She knew they'd both regret it in the morning, but it would be nice to feel like a married woman just once in her life.

THE FOLLOWING MORNING, no matter what aches she felt, Sadie got out of bed just before dawn as usual. Dressing in the darkness of their bedroom, she quietly slipped out of the room and down the stairs to fix breakfast. It was Saturday, and the children were still sleeping, and there was no real reason to wake them so early.

She decided to make pancakes and bacon for breakfast, knowing that the entire family would enjoy the delicious treat. As always, she made the bacon first, so there would be oil for the pancakes to cook in. If the children still weren't up when breakfast was done, she'd put it away for them.

The pot of coffee and bacon were done when Stanley got to the bottom of the stairs. "I'll do the chores," he said. She didn't know if he looked at her or not, because she certainly couldn't look at him.

By the time he was back from doing the morning chores, breakfast was finished, and Rachel had come downstairs and set the table. Sadie was terribly happy to have the child to act as a buffer on this morning.

"Were Steven and Charlotte awake yet?" Sadie asked.

Rachel shook her head. "They sleep late now that they don't go to Granny's every day."

"This is very true." Sadie and Rachel had become closer and closer during the month they'd spent together, and now Rachel went to Sadie with every little thought that flitted through her head. Sadie had never realized how much she'd enjoy a relationship with a girl Rachel's age.

"You know Tommy Jenkins?" Rachel asked.

"I've heard you mention him a time or two. And his mother is part of the quilting circle."

"He's been chasing me around at recess and pulling my braid," Rachel said. "I keep telling him to stop, but he won't. And when I spit on him, Miss Smith yelled at me."

Sadie did her best to keep her face straight. Spitting seemed very appropriate to Sadie, but she had a feeling the teacher wouldn't be as happy about it as she was. "Do you want me to talk to his mother?"

Rachel considered. "No, because he'd say I was a big baby for going to my ma and complaining. He's a thorn in my side, Ma!"

It was the first time any of the children had called her Ma, and Sadie stood for a moment with her eyes closed, just savoring the moment. What could be better than having children choose to call her Ma? If there was anything Sadie certainly couldn't think of what it would be.

"I understand that. He sounds like a real troublemaker."

"Tommy Jenkins is the kind of boy that you just want to push down, even though you know the teacher will be angry. Of course, Miss Smith is always angry."

"Oh, that can't be true! I've met her and she seemed very sweet!"

"Not when the boys put a frog in her desk. Or flung the erasers at each other. Or even when they used a tack and pinned Jennifer Scott's braids to the top of the desk behind her." Rachel shook her head. "She even makes the boys standing in the corner!"

"It sounds like she needs to have the boys stand in the corner. They misbehave like hooligans!" Sadie couldn't imagine trying to teach an unruly classroom.

Rachel sighed. "They really do. The girls are much better behaved, except when I spit on Tommy. Teacher made me stand in the corner that time, even though I told her I only did it to get Tommy to quit chasing me around the playground!"

Sadie shook her head. "Well, I don't think you should have been punished for just spitting on him after he'd chased you all over. It just isn't fair."

"That's what I told Miss Smith. I'm tired of her not punishing the boys when they start problems."

"What problems are the boys starting?" Stanley asked.

Rachel bit her lip. "I don't want you to be mad at me, Pa."

"You can tell Sadie about the problem, but you can't tell me?" He looked perplexed.

"She understands. It's a woman problem. Right, Sadie?"

Sadie bit her lip before answering. "I think we should probably tell your pa."

"You do?"

"I really do."

Rachel looked at her father. "Tommy Jenkins has been chasing me all around the playground at recess time. He wouldn't stop when I asked him to stop, so I had to spit on him."

Stanley shook his head. "You had to, did you?"

"You know I did, Pa. No one else was going to do anything about him, so I did."

"I suppose you had to. Did Miss Smith find out about you spitting on him?"

"Well, just as I spit, she stepped outside to call us in for class. She made me stand in the corner for hours and hours!"

"I doubt it was hours and hours. I don't know how I would have reacted if I'd seen a little girl spit on a boy." Stanley shook his head, more amused than anything. He was proud his daughter was standing up for herself on the playground, even if spitting was involved. He couldn't tell her that, of course, but he wanted to pat her on the back.

Rachel sighed dramatically. "Well, I'll tell you one thing right now! I will never marry Tommy Jenkins, even though I thought he was the nicest boy in class. Now I know better."

Sadie couldn't handle the conversation for another minute. For fear she would burst into laughter in front of Rachel, she hurried into the kitchen as if she'd forgotten something. While there, she poured two cups of coffee, and when Stanley joined her, she handed him one.

Forgetting who she was talking to for a moment, she said, "If you ever chase me, I'll spit on you twice. I'll have to!"

Stanley had just taken a sip of coffee and spit it right back out into his cup. "Sometimes, I just don't know what to do with her!" He chuckled softly.

Sadie started laughing as well. Both of them put their cups down because they were shaking so hard, they were afraid to spill. Stanley grabbed her and pulled her to him, hugging her tightly. So, they stood in the kitchen, embracing and laughing.

Rachel walked into the kitchen and stared at them for a moment before shaking her head. "Parents are strange." She left the room and went back to the table to finish setting it.

"Oh! You grabbed me. I should spit on you." Sadie acted like she was gathering saliva in her mouth to spit, and they both laughed harder.

Stanley finally got himself under control and shook his head. "I'm glad you're with me to help me parent. I don't think I'd have been nearly amused if I'd had to have that conversation on my own." He leaned down and softly brushed his lips against hers.

At first, Sadie was so surprised she didn't respond, but then she wrapped her arms around him and kissed him back for all she was worth. Maybe he had realized it was her when they'd made love during the night.

When he stepped back, she cleared her throat awkwardly. "I'm going to put the extra pancakes between two plates for when the little ones wake up."

Stanley watched her return to making breakfast with a small smile on his face. Somehow, Sadie was becoming important to him. He hadn't meant for it to happen, but her kindness toward the children, and her always taking care of his needs first made him think perhaps she was exactly what his family had needed.

When he'd woken during the night to find her in his arms, he hadn't been able to control his feelings. He didn't know if she even remembered it happening, but he hoped he could talk her into making their marriage a real one, so it could happen often.

They had their breakfast, and while they ate, they talked about unimportant things. "What will you do now that harvest is over?" Sadie asked.

"I like to plow the fields to ready them for next year. I plow them again then, but it just seems to me as if things grow better if the ground is plowed twice. I did really well with my potato crop this year, so I do believe I'll be doing more potatoes and less corn next year."

"I hope you saved some of the potatoes for us and didn't send them all to market," Sadie said. "I've noticed we all like our potatoes around here."

"I saved two hundred pounds in burlap sacks. I just haven't gotten them into the cellar yet."

"Maybe I'll make fried chicken and mashed potatoes for supper tonight. How does that sound?" She rarely asked for opinions when she decided to make something, but she felt lighter and happier today.

Stanley nodded. "I love your fried chicken. You put some kind of spice on it that my ma never used. And your chicken gravy is one of the most delicious things I've ever put into my mouth."

Sadie laughed softly. "I sure do feel like my cooking is something special around here. We always had someone to cook for us in the boarding house where I lived while I worked at the mill. I haven't really done any cooking since the orphanage."

Rachel grinned. "I like your chicken and gravy too, Ma."

Sadie felt herself tearing up. It made her so happy to think that Rachel was already wanting to call her Ma. She was choosing to show affection with the term, rather than being forced to. It felt good.

Stanley frowned at Rachel's use of Ma for Sadie. Did that mean his daughter was forgetting about Charlotte? He certainly hoped not. But he wanted his children to love Sadie as their Ma. But he didn't. It was hard to know what he wanted at all.

"I think I'm going to take the day off today, and we're all going to drive out to the lake. It's too chilly to swim, but we can pick up some nice rocks. I've heard that Miss Smith is going to paint rocks with the children. Seems odd to me, but I'll happily help." Stanley looked at Sadie. "How does going to the lake and having a picnic lunch sound?"

Sadie nodded, a smile on her face. "If sandwiches are all right, I can get those ready quickly."

"Sandwiches are fine. I'll go and butcher one of the chickens while you make the sandwiches. It'll take a few hours to get to the lake, so we'll all be hungry again when we get there."

Rachel looked between the two adults at the table, a huge smile on her face. "We're really going to the lake, Papa?"

Stanley nodded, smiling at Rachel. She hadn't called him Papa in a good long while, and it felt good when she did. "We're really going to the lake. While Sadie gets the sandwiches ready, would you run upstairs and wake your brother and sister?"

Rachel nodded emphatically. "I'd be happy to!"

Sadie looked at Stanley. "Remember we'll need to do the dishes before we go as well."

Stanley nodded. "Rachel help with the dishes, and then go upstairs to wake Charlotte and Steven." He wiped his mouth with the napkin in front of him and hurried outside to get the chicken butchered.

Sadie and Rachel worked together to clear the table and wash the dishes. Rachel enjoyed wiping, so they were a good team. When that task was done, Rachel ran up the stairs to wake her siblings, while Sadie made sandwiches for them all.

She cut yesterday's bread into slices and took out some roast beef they'd had for supper two nights ago. Adding a tiny bit of gravy to the inside of each sandwich, she hoped everyone would enjoy them. She made eight sandwiches in all, knowing she'd only eat one, but there was a good chance Stanley would eat two or three.

They had no picnic basket, so she put all of the food into a pillowcase and added plates for the children. She and Stanley could eat their sandwiches without plates.

She put a jar of water for each of them into the bag as well, carefully wrapping each jar with a kitchen towel so as to keep them from breaking and banging against each other.

Rachel came downstairs with both of the younger children, and Sadie was happy to see she'd been able to persuade Steven to wear his pants. Now that he had choices, he did much better when he had to leave the house.

Stanley brought in the chicken he'd slaughtered. "I hitched up the wagon as well. I'm ready when you are."

Sadie thought she might just be more excited than the children as they all went outside and got into the wagon. She looked at Stanley. "Would Charlotte do better if I held her, or in the back with the others?"

"Hold her. At least to start with. She may get tired of being held and want to go in the back, but let's start out holding her."

As they drove, Stanley pointed out houses of people in town, so she would have a better idea of who lived where. She looked around, but she knew she'd never remember. She wasn't good with directions at all.

They could just barely see the lake up ahead and Sadie got excited. "I think I may just be more excited than the children."

He laughed. "I'm more excited than the children. I'm glad we can all share this day."

"Me too." Stanley had worked most Sundays since she'd arrived. This was really the first time they were going anywhere or doing anything as a family. She was starting to feel like maybe they'd all accepted her as family now. It was a good feeling.

Chapter Nine

As a woman who had lived on the shores of the Atlantic Ocean, it seemed odd to Sadie how very beautiful the lake was. It was calmer than the ocean, but so much smaller.

"There are Indian legends about a monster that lives in the lake. I've never seen it, but I've heard a few say they have. It's fun to hear people talk about it." Stanley set the brake and jumped down from the wagon, walking around to help Sadie down. He grabbed her by the waist and held her against him for a moment, causing her to slide down to the ground against his body.

Sadie was flushed when he was done, but she said nothing, simply moving to the back of the wagon to take Charlotte. The girl immediately headed for the water. Sadie chased after her. "The water is too cold, Charlotte! I don't want you to get sick."

Charlotte pouted but walked toward her brother, who was sitting in the sand.

"Rachel, will you watch your brother and sister and make sure they don't go in the lake? I'm going to get our picnic blanket out and set the food out."

Rachel nodded. "Yes, Ma!"

Stanley reached into the back of the wagon for the blanket and pillowcase full of food. "I should have given you an oilcloth bag for the picnic. I don't know what I was thinking."

Sadie let her eyes drift to his brown ones, and she realized she was seeing something in his eyes that hadn't been there before. Was he really developing feelings for her?

"This works. Next time I'll ask for oilcloth." Sadie reached for the blanket, but he had it tucked under one arm. He spread it onto the ground while Sadie set the plates out for the children and each jar of water.

Then she handed Stanley his sandwich. "No plate for me?"

Sadie shook her head as his fingers stroked hers. "No, I thought we could eat without plates, and the bag would be lighter."

"Good choice!" She looked over at the three children playing with the rocks on the side of the lake. "Come eat!"

The children hurried toward her, each of them sitting at a plate. Stanley bowed his head and prayed over their meal, thanking God for sending just the right new ma for his children.

While they ate, Stanley's eyes remained on Sadie. He wished he'd left the children with his mother, so he could be more affectionate with Sadie. She was exactly who he needed in his life, and he hadn't even realized anything was missing.

Rachel talked about school and how she was sure Miss Smith hated her after she spat at Tommy, even though he deserved it. Sadie was only half listening. Stanley's hand was holding hers as they each ate their sandwich one handed.

After the picnic, the children went to find rocks to take to the school while Sadie cleaned up their mess and put it all in the back of the wagon. All except the picnic blanket which she shared with Stanley.

To her surprise, he leaned down and kissed her once again. There wasn't really anyone else near them, but anyone could come along. She didn't think Stanley would like public displays of affection.

After a moment, she completely lost herself in the kiss. The sounds of the children playing faded away, and her world narrowed to the man sitting with her.

The sound of another wagon made Stanley realize there were others around. He lifted his head, looking down at her lips, moist with his kisses. He turned to see who it was and smiled. "It's Pastor Jed and his wife, Hannah. And their children."

Sadie turned toward the wagon, wanting to scream. She was having a nice romantic outing with the man she loved, and the Scotts should have known to stay away. Instead of airing her thoughts, she raised a hand in greeting. "Hannah! It's good to see you!" Their oldest child was a girl who looked to be around fifteen or sixteen. And the youngest was a babe in Hannah's arms.

The Scotts walked over to them, and Hannah asked, "Do you mind if we put our blanket beside yours?"

"Not at all," Sadie lied. "The children have wandered off."

Jed spread their blanket out, and Hannah sat down on it. "Meg, you may go and find Rachel," Hannah said.

Meg hurried off to find her friend while Hannah sat. "I meant to bring a picnic, but we decided to eat at the boarding house instead. Margaret is the best cook in the entire Bear Lake Valley."

"I beg to differ," Stanley said. "Sadie is the best cook in the valley."

Hannah looked at Sadie with wide eyes. "Usually, he says his mother is the best cook around. You must be very good."

Sadie shrugged, a bit embarrassed after the praise. "I hadn't cooked since I was fourteen before this last month. I find I remember what to do, and I enjoy it so much. Rachel is learning to cook as well."

Hannah smiled. "Thankfully, Ellen is a good cook," she said, nodding to her oldest child.

"What is your older son's name?" Sadie asked. She knew Ellen and Meg. But she didn't know the name of either of the boys.

"Joshua. And the baby is William."

"Your children are very spread out!" Sadie said.

Hannah nodded. "Thankfully. I don't know if I could handle three as young as yours are. Do you want more?"

Sadie wasn't sure how to answer. It wasn't something she and Stanley had discussed, and she'd thought it wasn't a possibility. "I think I would."

Stanley nodded. "Sadie is already proving to be an amazing mother. I think she'd do well with children of her own."

Sadie turned to look for the children, and saw that Rachel and Meg had the other two choosing rocks.

Hannah laughed softly. "The children are fine. Though if you're worried, I could have Ellen go down and watch over them."

Sadie shook her head. "No, I trust the girls."

They stayed for another hour after the picnic and then decided to head home. "I still have to make supper," Sadie said, though she'd enjoyed the picnic as well as her time with the Scotts.

The two little ones slept in the back of the wagon on the way back to Clover Creek. Rachel seemed to be fighting sleep, but she wanted to prove how grown up she was. Much to grown up for naps.

"I had a lovely time today," Sadie said softly. "Thank you for suggesting we spend a whole day together."

Stanley smiled, putting the leads into his left hand, so he could wind the fingers of his right hand through hers. "It's just such a beautiful day, and there aren't crowds at the lake at this time of year."

"The lake is gorgeous. I thought I'd be let down after living on the ocean for the past six years, but I was in awe. Though I never did see the monster you mentioned."

"I haven't either. But I'll keep looking every time I go."

"Good! Never stop looking for monsters should be our family motto."

He chuckled. "I like that. Whether we find them or not, looking for them is fun."

When they returned home, Stanley carried all three sleeping children into the house one at a time, depositing them in their beds. Sadie went straight to the kitchen to pluck the chicken and get it ready for supper.

She was working on peeling a small mountain of potatoes when he walked up behind her, wrapping his arms around her waist. "The children are all sleeping," he whispered.

She smiled. "Good. Then I can cook supper in peace." She finished the potato she was peeling, and he took the knife from her and spun her around for his kiss.

Standing close together, he finally raised his head and rested his forehead against hers. "I'm looking forward to bedtime tonight."

Sadie blushed. "You seem to have your mind on one thing and one thing only today," she said.

"With such a beautiful woman beside him, how could I think of anything else?"

"Would you mind more children?" she asked. She knew it probably wasn't the time, but they were talking about the act that made babies, so she wasn't sure why she couldn't ask.

"I wouldn't mind at all. I hope we'll have at least one or two together, but I wouldn't complain if we ended up with an even dozen."

Sadie laughed. "I think we'd have to add on to the house for that many!"

"We could sure do that!" he said. "I happen to enjoy building. Around here, we tend to help each other with building projects to get them done quicker. We got used to relying on each other on the trail, and it just never stopped."

There was a knock on the door, and Stanley reluctantly let her go to see who was there. When he opened the door, he saw Grace and Jack standing there. "Come in! I don't know if Sadie was expecting you."

"She wasn't," Grace said. "I just needed to see my best friend for a few minutes."

"She's in the kitchen cooking supper."

"Then I do believe I'll help her."

Sadie was surprised to see Grace. They usually saw each other for tea once per week and on Sundays at church. "Is everything all right?"

Grace shrugged and burst into tears. "I don't know. I'm an emotional wreck. The baby is weighing heavily on me, but I'm sure I'm going to be pregnant for at least another ten years."

Sadie smiled. "You know better. What can I do to help?"

"Nothing. I just needed to see you." Grace sighed, picking up a knife and a potato and helping her friend. "How's the marriage going?" she asked softly, so the men in the other room wouldn't hear.

"I think we've turned a corner," Sadie responded. "We went on a picnic to the lake today. Stanley took the whole day off work so we could be together. He's never done that before."

"And are you two intimate?"

"Grace! You have no right asking questions like that!" Even best friends should have some secrets between them.

"Hey, I'm having a hard day. I think you should tell me."

Sadie looked down at the potato in her hand and softly whispered, "Yes, we are."

"That's wonderful! I'm happy it's working out for you and your new family."

"I am too. I didn't dare dream it would be this good so soon after the wedding. The children are polite and respectful. Stanley is very attentive and kind. He's always complimenting my cooking. I think this was the perfect family for me, and now we're talking about children that are ours."

"We must have daughters at the same time so they can be best friends just as we are."

Sadie shook her head. "I don't know how we could make that work, but I'm willing if you are."

"I don't know," Grace said. "I think this is going to be my last baby. I don't know if I can go through this again."

"You're feeling very dramatic today, aren't you?"

"Yes! That's what I've been trying to tell you."

Sadie dropped the last potato into the water and set the pot onto the stove so they could start boiling. Then she mixed flour and a few spices and started the chicken.

Grace stood and watched. "Who taught you to make chicken that way?"

Sadie shrugged. "We learned to fry chicken at the orphanage, but I've been experimenting with spices to find just what I like."

"You're a much more natural cook than I am," Grace said, shaking her head. "I might need to come over and get cooking lessons from you."

"I wouldn't mind, but we were taught by the same person."

"Oh, Sadie. Can I start coming over during the week? At least until the baby is born. I feel like I'm losing my mind with as much time as I spend at home alone."

Sadie had never seen Grace be so needy. "Yes, of course, you may. I don't do anything exciting except cook, clean, and sew all day, but if you want to join, you are welcome to do so."

"What time is Rachel gone for school?"

"She leaves about eight-fifteen most mornings. And by then Stanley is out working as well." Sadie flipped the chicken in the iron skillet. "Oh, I should warn you. Steven only wears nightshirts around the house."

"He's not running around naked anymore?" Grace looked surprised.

"The nightshirts are our compromise. He can wear them at home any time he wants, but if we leave, he has to wear pants."

Grace shook her head. "I've never seen a child hate clothes as much as Steven."

"Neither have I, but as long as he's not running around naked, I have no problem with it."

Sadie finished with the chicken and set it onto a plate. Then she took the drippings and made gravy. "Do you think you'll come in the mornings?"

"I think I probably will. If you really don't mind that is."

"I'm surprised you don't want to visit Sarah. She at least knows what it feels like to be pregnant and can give you good advice."

"I don't want advice. I don't want people rubbing my stomach. I want people to leave me alone and act as if I'm not expecting." Grace plopped down in a kitchen chair. "Why doesn't anyone understand that?"

"No idea," Sadie said. "I'd be happy to do what you need to help you feel better though. But we may end up spending lots of time sewing and knitting. I want to make hats, scarves, and mittens for each of the children for Christmas."

"I could help with that," Grace said. "It'll take my mind off everything."

"What are you afraid of, Grace?" Sadie knew her friend well enough to know she was hiding something.

"Childbirth," Grace all but wailed. "What if I die? Who will take care of my baby?"

Sadie finished mashing the potatoes and then went to sit with Grace, taking her hand. "If you die in childbirth, then I'll take care of your child while Jack works."

"You would?"

Sadie nodded her head, laughing. "You know I'd do anything in the world for you. I always have, and I always will."

Grace pursed her lips and then nodded. "I guess Sarah could take care of the baby, but everything's just been so difficult lately. I love Sarah, but she's not you."

"I'm so glad you found a reason for me to move out here to join you. I want to be a big part of your life like I always have been."

"Thank you."

Chapter Ten

Grace and Jack left just before supper, even though Sadie invited them to join them. Grace seemed to be in much better spirits, and Sadie hoped she would stay that way, but her door would always be open for her friend.

They had to wake the children to eat supper. The fresh air at the lake had apparently exhausted all three of them.

Rachel stopped in front of the table and immediately started crying.

"What's wrong?" Sadie asked. It was the first time she'd seen the child cry.

"You set the table without me!" Rachel wailed.

"Oh, sweetie. I only did it so you could get some sleep. I knew how tired you were."

"But I want you to know you can't do without me, so you won't send me away to an orphanage."

Sadie's eyes opened wide, and she sat down, pulling the girl toward her so they could talk eye-to-eye. "I would never send you away. I love you, Rachel, and I'm proud to call you my daughter."

"But...one of the girls at school told me that when a ma dies, the new ma that comes sends all the old ma's children to an orphanage. I thought if I acted really good and always helped around the house, you wouldn't send us away."

Sadie pulled the girl to her, holding her close and patting her back. "Whoever told you that is a liar. I would never send any of you away. And not only because I love you. Do you know why else?"

Rachel shook her head, her braids hitting Sadie in the face. "Because your pa loves you so much, he wouldn't know what to do if you weren't here. Why I think he'd spend all day in the barn crying."

Rachel giggled. "Pas don't cry!"

Stanley had watched the entire conversation between Sadie and Rachel, and he knew he needed to comment. "I would cry all the time if I lost you. What would I do without my favorite daughters?"

Rachel looked over her shoulder at her father. "Really Pa?"

"Really."

After supper, Rachel helped with the dishes and then they all went into the parlor together. "We should play hide the thimble," Sadie suggested. She'd spent hours and hours trying to find the thimble the matron had hidden when she was a little girl.

"How, Ma?" Rachel asked.

Sadie explained the rules and had the children cover their eyes while she hid the thimble. Then she sat on the sofa snuggled closely with Stanley while the children looked everywhere for the thimble.

"Thank you for talking to Rachel the way you did. I know she's still insecure, but I think she'll be lots better when she feels like you want her here."

"I don't know why she'd think I wouldn't want her here! I tell her every day what a wonderful girl she is. Even when she tells me she had to spit on a boy."

He grinned at that. "I have laughed more with you in the past month than I have since my father died."

"But that happened years and years ago," Sadie said. "Surely you and Charlotte laughed together."

He shook his head. "She wasn't easily amused. She was more of a sullen woman than anything else. I didn't realize it til after we were married, but she wasn't nearly as happy as you are."

Sadie thought that seemed strange. The woman had known she had Stanley's love. Sadie was so desperate to have his love that she was settling for passion. "But she knew you loved her."

"Knowing you're loved doesn't automatically mean you're happy," Stanley told her. "I love the children, and Rachel feels very insecure. I love you, and I haven't seen you dancing about with happiness."

Sadie's jaw dropped. "You don't love me!"

"I think I know my own feelings." Stanley shook his head. "Do you really think I'd have made love to you last night if I didn't love you?"

"I thought you mistook me for Charlotte." Sadie looked down at her hands.

"And you let it happen anyway?" He studied her curiously.

"Well, I know I love you, and if it was the only time we were ever going to share physical love, I wasn't going to stop you."

He blinked a few times. "You love me? I've been so grumpy with you, I find that hard to believe."

"I understood why you were grumpy. I'd have been grumpy too!" Sadie took a deep breath and spilled her guts. "Coming here to marry you was the scariest thing I'd ever done. After meeting you, I knew I'd fall in love with you quickly, and I never expected my love to be returned. I thought about calling everything off, but I decided to concentrate on my love for the children, which I knew would help me not think about you so much." She shrugged. "It worked except in the middle of the night when you treated me like a special blanket."

He chuckled. "I do love you. I held you in my sleep because I was afraid you wouldn't let me while I was awake. And because I didn't want to fall in love with you, but that's flown right out the window."

She smiled, scooting even closer to him and initiating a kiss. "I'm glad you're my husband, Stanley Gabriel."

The children came in and saw them kissing. They didn't realize that Rachel took the hands of her younger siblings and led them from the room.

Epilogue

Three years later, Sadie held her fifth(you know she counts the first three as hers) child in her arms—a daughter. She smiled as she thought about what Grace had said about them each having a daughter to be best friends with the other.

Grace had her first daughter just a week before. They'd both started out with boys, and both of them were pleased to have had healthy children, but now?

Stanley walked into the bedroom to check on her. "Do you need anything?" He smiled at the little girl his wife held. They now had five children, and he couldn't imagine being any happier than he was at that very moment.

"I want to send a note to Grace. Would you take it to her?"

"Of course. Are you sure you'll be okay here with just you and the baby?"

"Oh please. Rachel is within calling distance and ready to do anything to make her little sister happy." She reached out and took his hand. "Get me a pencil and paper, would you?"

Stanley came back a moment later with what she'd asked for, and he stood and waited while she wrote her note.

My dearest friend Grace,

I want to inform you that we've made your dream come true. My daughter arrived a few hours ago, just one week younger than yours. They will be best friends all their days, and they will grow up knowing they always have a confidante.

All my love,

Sadie

Stanley took the note and folded it in half without reading it. He'd learned a lot about having a best female friend from Sadie and Grace. The two women seemed to want to live in one another's apron pockets.

"I'll be back in a short while. Take care of Elizabeth."

Sadie stared down at her beautiful child. "Always."

Sign up for instant notification of all of Kirsten's New Releases here[1].

And

For a complete list of Kirsten's works head to her website wwww.kirstenandmorganna.com

---

[1]. http://www.kirstenandmorganna.com/newsletter